ADJOURNED

ALSO BY LEE GOLDBERG

King City
The Walk
Watch Me Die
McGrave
Three Ways to Die
Fast Track

The Ian Ludlow Thrillers
True Fiction
Killer Thriller
Fake Truth

The Eve Ronin Series
Lost Hills
Bone Canyon
Gated Prey
Movieland

The Fox & O'Hare Series (coauthored with Janet Evanovich)
Pros & Cons (novella)
The Shell Game (novella)
The Heist
The Chase
The Job
The Scam
The Pursuit

The Diagnosis Murder Series
The Silent Partner
The Death Merchant

The Shooting Script
The Waking Nightmare
The Past Tense
The Dead Letter
The Double Life
The Last Word

The Monk Series
Mr. Monk Goes to the Firehouse
Mr. Monk Goes to Hawaii
Mr. Monk and the Blue Flu
Mr. Monk and the Two Assistants
Mr. Monk in Outer Space
Mr. Monk Goes to Germany
Mr. Monk Is Miserable
Mr. Monk and the Dirty Cop
Mr. Monk in Trouble
Mr. Monk Is Cleaned Out
Mr. Monk on the Road
Mr. Monk on the Couch
Mr. Monk on Patrol
Mr. Monk Is a Mess
Mr. Monk Gets Even

The Charlie Willis Series
My Gun Has Bullets
Dead Space

The Dead Man Series (coauthored with William Rabkin)
Face of Evil
Ring of Knives (with James Daniels)
Hell in Heaven
The Dead Woman (with David McAfee)
The Blood Mesa (with James Reasoner)

ADJOURNED

LEE GOLDBERG

CUTTING EDGE

ISBN-13: 978-1-954840-81-2

Published by
Cutting Edge Books
PO Box 8212
Calabasas, CA 91372
www.cuttingedgebooks.com

To Kelly, for living with it, and to Karen,
for listening to it.

ADJOURNED

PROLOGUE

The little girl in pigtails scrambled onto Santa Claus's lap. Old St. Nicholas, stark naked, wrapped his arms around her and, with a hearty "Ho ho ho," asked her what he could give her for Christmas.

Santa gaped joyfully at the girl sitting stiff-backed on his fleshy legs. His heavy hairless chest lolled on the swell of his stomach, his pale skin flushed baby's-bottom pink. The girl stared blankly at the brightly wrapped empty gift boxes that cluttered the floor around them. Behind Santa and the girl, a Christmas tree strewn with blinking lights glowed against a wood facade paneled with red Masonite strips designed to look like brick.

"Don't leer so much, Santa," Wesley Saputo groaned, combing his hand through his brown hair and sharing an irritated smirk with Lyle Franken, the chunky cameraman. "We're looking for fatherly warmth here."

Santa squinted against the bright lights, trying to see Saputo in the darkness behind them. A bead of sweat rolled down Santa's cherubic face.

"Sure, I can do that," Santa sputtered, shifting uncomfortably in his seat, a splinter of wood from the hastily built throne pricking his butt.

The girl reflexively clutched at a roll of flesh on his stomach to steady herself.

"Good, good. That's why I pay you," Saputo said wearily. Then, more softly, he asked: "Okay, Cassie, how are you doing?"

The ten-year-old girl squirmed at the mention of her name. Her usual exuberance had been sanded down to shyness by her nakedness, the strange way the man in the Santa Claus beard and cap looked at her, the heat and glare of the bright movie lights.

"Fine," she mumbled, toying with one of the red bows in her cherry-red hair. "When do we get ice cream and go to Disneyland?"

"Not long, Cassie. Don't you want to be a star?" said the voice behind the lights.

"Uh-huh."

"Okay," Saputo crooned. "Then let's do like I told you. Be nice to Santa the way I said."

Saputo heard footsteps approaching slowly behind him in the darkness of the warehouse. Glancing over his shoulder, he saw a tall figure wearing a long dark blue Navy peacoat with the collar turned up against his neck. Saputo felt a tremor in his chest. *Tice.*

Saputo swatted Franken's side. Franken, who also doubled as production designer and throne builder, turned from the viewfinder and followed Saputo's gaze.

"Good afternoon, gentlemen," said the man, wiry and thin, as he emerged from the shadows and glided toward Saputo and Franken like the surf crawling up the sand.

"Shit," Franken groaned, turning back to the camera.

"Keep shooting," Saputo quietly told Franken and, with anxiety fluttering in his chest, approached Tice.

Tice always made Saputo nervous. It was Tice's face that did it. His features seemed to Saputo like sharp cuts of flesh carved by the quick, slashing strokes of a razor. Tice had narrow slits for eyes, a jagged scar for a smile, a needlelike nose, and strands of stubby black hair that coated the top of his skull like a thin layer of paint.

And it was the way Tice spoke. No matter how loud or hushed his voice, Tice's words always sounded to Saputo like a whisper.

Yet it was always audible, never muted, stealthily enveloping any conversation. A vocal oil slick.

"Mr. Orlock is looking forward to more of your work," Tice said, looking past Saputo to the Christmas set. Saputo glanced back and saw Santa caressing Cassie's thigh.

"So am I." Saputo nodded.

"He wants you to know it's nice to have you back," Tice said emotionlessly. He apparently didn't share Orlock's enthusiasm.

"It's nice to be back," Saputo agreed. It's nice not having my dong tied to some fucking penile plethysmograph, he thought. It's nice not getting electrocuted every time I see a sweet, hairless cunt and the machine tells some jerk-off shrink I've got a hard-on. It's nice being *free.*

Without Mr. Orlock's help, Saputo knew, he might still be in that gray nuthouse, where everything smelled like rubbing alcohol.

"He is expecting a lot of product in a very short time. You *can* come through, can't you, Wesley?"

"Sure, no problem. Just keep the money coming."

"But there *is* a problem, Wesley," Tice replied melodically. "You haven't been keeping up your side of the bargain."

Saputo's heart skipped a beat. "What do you mean? This picture will be done soon. It's on budget. What's the problem?"

"Where did you get the girl, Wesley?" Tice inquired softly.

Saputo saw Santa spread Cassie's legs apart. "A runaway. I, ah, found her cowering under the Santa Monica pier," Saputo said in a matter-of-fact tone, watching the scene unfold in front of the cameras. He had taken her here for the night, and then, this morning, Saputo tied Cassie's hair into pigtails and took her to the International House of Pancakes.

While she ate her breakfast, a pancake "happy face" with a pineapple smile and whipped-cream hair, Saputo told her how he wanted to take her to the biggest, bestest ice cream parlor on earth. Then to Disneyland, where they would stay for days. All she had to do was be in a movie about Christmas.

You love Christmas, don't you? he had asked her. Santa Claus will be in it. He'll have lots of presents. All you have to do is have a good time and tickle Santa. Then you can have all the ice cream you want and then we'll play together for as long as you like.

She said it sounded fun and asked for a glass of chocolate milk.

"That wasn't wise, Wesley," Tice said, breaking into Saputo's thoughts. "You're not being very smart."

Saputo shrugged, shifting his attention back to Tice. "Got a better idea?"

Tice's gaze stabbed into him. "I'll get you the children, you make the movies. That's the bargain. It wouldn't be healthy for you to get caught again."

"Yeah, sure." Saputo held up his hand, pushing at the air between them, anxiety dancing in his chest again. "Take it easy, no problem. I don't want to go back to prison or the hospital again."

"That isn't where you'd be going, Wesley." Tice grinned and walked back into the shadows.

Asshole. Saputo trudged back to the set.

The camera was still whirring, Lyle Franken's eye glued to the viewfinder. Franken's gaze narrowed on Cassie's pigtails ... soft, tuggable pigtails that bounced with every movement of her head. Franken liked girls best when they wore their hair that way. And the girls sometimes liked him. They liked Franken because his short stature and his rolls of fat gave him the accordion shape of a cartoon character crushed by a huge boulder.

Franken saw Santa's eyes bulge with pleasure and wished he could be in that makeshift throne with Cassie buried between his legs. *Santa's Little Helper,* Franken was certain, was going to be a classic film.

Saputo stepped behind Franken and off to one side, sharing similar thoughts. But, unlike Franken, Saputo *would* get his turn. Oh yes, he certainly would.

"Great, Cassie, just great." Saputo grinned, his tobacco-stained teeth sticky with saliva. There were no fucking machines to zap his hard-ons away now.

"Cut," Saputo said heavily. Santa Claus held Cassie against his heaving chest. Her eyes were vacant, her face sickly pale.

Franken stepped back from the camera and patted Saputo on the back. "The lab boys should be able to get this off in three days. This is going to be a big one, Wesley, I can feel it in my—"

"I know where you can feel it," Saputo interrupted, staring at Cassie, a grin spreading on his face. Franken's chirpy coughs of laughter spilled out in a rush as Saputo went to Cassie and picked her up off of Santa's lap.

She was dead weight in his arms. Pliant.

Saputo swallowed dryly. "Okay, boys, it's a wrap. You guys clean up here."

Franken jealously watched Saputo head toward the warehouse door with Cassie. "Be gentle, Wesley."

"I always am." The door closed behind him.

Sgt. Ronald Shaw had seen a lot of dead bodies. Not many made him cry. He struggled to keep his tears away from the half-dozen other officers huddled in the pounding rain as they stood staring at the bloated corpse of a ten-year-old girl.

Even in death, lying in the mud beside the raging waters surging down the drainage canal, Shaw could see her beauty. Shaw looked at her vibrant red hair, caked with dirt, and her face, now a lifeless pearl white, and imagined the way she must have glowed when she smiled. Shaw couldn't stop staring. The water that had washed her up from God knows where lapped gently against her, tossing her tiny pigtails.

"Sergeant Shaw?" a voice from behind him ventured carefully. The black homicide detective, stirred from his thoughts, looked back, wiping his eyes with the back of his hand.

A snout-nosed man hiding under the biggest brown umbrella he had ever seen approached him. Shaw, no longer lost in the emotion of the moment, felt the stinging wetness of his rain-soaked clothes against his skin. In Shaw's rush to get here from the office he had left his umbrella drip-drying in the garbage can beside his desk.

The man offered his black-gloved hand to Shaw and held his umbrella over them both. "Sergeant Clive Barer, Sexually Exploited Child Unit, Juvenile Division. We've met once before."

Shaw reached out and shook Barer's hand, the leather glove slick in Shaw's wet grasp. "It's been a long time, Clive. Five years."

Barer shrugged. "I wish we weren't meeting again this way." He took a step toward the overpass that stretched across the canal a few yards away and offered shelter from the downpour.

Shaw followed, glancing back at the girl, her neck bruised a teal blue where crushing hands had choked the air out of her. The rushing water beside her charged along the cement canal south into the distant, stark industrial wastelands of Commerce and Southgate.

"Who found her?" Shaw asked, looking forward and trudging alongside Barer through the mud.

"A guy on the freeway lost a suitcase off the top of his car. It landed down here. You know, one of those Samsonite things," Barer said, lowering his umbrella as they walked under the overpass. "Anyway, he came down to get it and found her."

The roar of the rain drowned out the sound of the cars Shaw could feel rumbling on the San Bernardino Freeway overhead. Shaw shivered and wondered when he would see Noah's Ark sail down the canal.

"Do you know who she is?" Shaw asked.

"Yeah. Cassie Reed, ten years old, lived with her divorced mother in West LA. A week ago Cassie's mother gave the kid a spanking for not doing her chores and sent her to her room," he replied. "She never saw the kid again."

Barer cleared his throat. "Did you see the kid's neck?"

Shaw nodded.

"Familiar, isn't it?" Barer sighed.

"Yeah," Shaw said. "But I put Saputo behind bars. There's no way he could have done this."

Barer shook his head wearily. "He was released on parole two months ago."

CHAPTER ONE

Listening to the Bowel Movement made Los Angeles Mayor Jed Stocker grimace. The tinny electronic sound and screeching lyrics blaring over the stereo speakers across the room made Stocker feel like he wasn't in his office but strapped into a dentist's chair having his teeth drilled.

Without Novocain.

An insistent pounding at the door, which at first Stocker thought was part of the song, gave him the excuse he needed to leave his desk and twist the stereo's volume down low.

"Come in," Stocker yelled gratefully, the last note of the song ringing in his ears.

Sgt. Ronald Shaw stepped in, closing the door behind him. "I got here as quickly as I could." He noticed the album cover for the Bowel Movement beside the stereo. It depicted a toilet, the open seat cover fanged like the mouth of a hungry shark, chasing a Ronald Reagan lookalike out of the bathroom. "I didn't know you liked that kind of music, sir."

Stocker removed the record from the turntable. "I don't. My son, Jed Jr., known as Faced to his fans, just became the lead singer of a new wave group. This is their latest album. I decided to give it a chance. He told me the only way to enjoy it is loud."

The mayor flung the record like a Frisbee into the garbage can beside his desk and clapped his hands together. "I think I've just discovered the only way to enjoy *that* record."

Shaw chuckled. "Why does he call himself Faced?"

"It's shorthand for shit-faced." Stocker walked back to his desk and settled into his high-backed leather chair, the city's seal on the wall behind him. "And on that point, I'd have to agree with him. The kid has so much crap in his veins he never knows night from day." He nodded in Shaw's direction. "Sit down, Sergeant."

Shaw took a seat facing Stocker, who was flanked on one side by the state flag and the national flag on the other. "What can I do for you, sir? Your message was rather vague."

Stocker scooted his chair forward and opened a file that was on the desk. "It's about your investigation into the murders of those young girls." He shuffled through the papers for a moment before finding the one he wanted. "Oh yes, here it is."

Leaning back in his chair, propping the file open in his lap, Stocker shot a scornful glance at Shaw. "Well, Sergeant, thanks to you, the city is being sued for three million dollars.'

"Look, Mayor—" Shaw began.

Stocker continued, raising his voice over Shaw's. "A trio of sharp Century City lawyers representing Wesley Saputo are charging you with harassment. They say he hasn't been able to move an inch without bumping into a badge."

"C'mon, sir, I'm only doing my job," Shaw insisted. "In the two weeks since we found Cassie Reed beside the canal, two more girls have been kidnapped, raped, and strangled. The murders fit Saputo's M.O. I've only been doing what any conscientious cop would do. I've brought him in for questioning, obtained a search warrant and gone through his house, and maintained constant surveillance."

Stocker shook his head. "I appreciate enthusiasm. As former police chief, and now as mayor, I expect my officers to take the extra step. But, Sergeant, you've gone too far."

Shaw felt his face flushing with anger. "What do you want me to do, let him go on raping and killing young girls?"

Shaw had seen it happen before. Men like Saputo are labeled mentally disordered sex offenders, sent to a cushy state hospital for a few years, and then put back on the street. Shaw didn't know who was sicker, Saputo or the shrinks who set him free.

"Don't smart-mouth me, Shaw," Stocker thundered. "You have to face reality. His lawyers say you don't have any evidence against him, not a single fingerprint and no semen match-up."

"I *know* it's Saputo," Shaw shot back. "True, we have no prints. But all of Saputo's victims were girls between the ages of ten and twelve. Same thing now. All of Saputo's victims were raped, sodomized, and strangled. Again, so are the new victims. We couldn't get a blood type off of Saputo's semen five years ago because he is a non-secreter. The person who raped these girls is also a non-secreter."

"So, to summarize, you don't have shit," Stocker stated, tossing the file onto his desk.

Shaw tapped the arm of his chair with his fingers, trying to keep cool. "I'll get the evidence, you can count on that. I'll make sure they put him behind bars forever."

"How are you going to do that?" Stocker asked. "Saputo's lawyers are going to seek a restraining order from Superior Court Judge Lewis Nile this afternoon and I think they'll get it. Any further attempts to bring Saputo in for questioning and the lawyers will haul us to court."

Stocker scowled. "Face it, you botched this one, Shaw. You came on too strong and now we can't get near him."

Shaw glared at Stocker. "Are you telling me to let this guy go?"

"No, I'm telling you to call Brett Macklin."

The words, like a sharp punch to the solar plexus, stole Shaw's breath. He stared at the mayor for a moment in disbelieving silence.

"I want these murders to stop, but I don't want Saputo and his lawyers getting a chance to give the press a show," Stocker explained. "I don't want Saputo turned into some kind of fucking martyr. The city doesn't need a slew of negative headlines screaming about police harassment."

"The city doesn't need a vigilante, either. Fighting crime with crime isn't the answer," Shaw cautioned. "Let's not make the situation any worse."

"How could it get any worse, Sergeant? You just got done telling me that Saputo is killing children. I'm telling you the LAPD can't get near him." Stocker held up his hands despairingly. "Do you have a better idea?"

"There has to be another way, a legal way," Shaw insisted.

"There is no other way," Stocker shouted. "I want Macklin on this. *Now.*"

He ran madly down the street, the World War I fighter plane riddling the asphalt on either side of him with bullets. The plane streaked across the cloudless sky above the office buildings, banked, and barreled down on him again, the gun turrets spitting slugs.

He dived onto a parked car, rolled across the hood, and fell onto the sidewalk behind it. Bullets chewed up the street toward the car. He flung himself forward as the bullets raked the car and punctured the gas tank.

The car exploded, ripping the air and hurling a pulsating ball of flame into the sky. The plane roared away, preparing to bank again.

He stood up, flames licking out for him, and pulled the Magnum out of his waistband.

"Fuck this," he mumbled, strolling into the street, shrouded by a veil of smoke. He stopped in the center of the street and straddled the broken white dividing line, daring the plane. "Come and get it."

The plane dropped down low and came for him.

The flames from the car sounded like a windstorm, the staccato beat of the bullets chipping away at the street a savage hail.

He raised his gun. The plane filled his vision. The engine's roar filled his ears. The bullets clamored for him.

He fired twice.

The plane vomited deep black smoke and curled sharply in a skyward arc, sputtered, and dived. Rocking uncontrollably, the plane glided unevenly toward the entrance of a parking structure behind him, as if it suddenly thought it was just a fancy Ford station wagon.

The plane's wings were ripped away as it skidded through the entranceway into the darkness on a carpet of sparks and smoke. A split second later, an explosion tore through the structure, the building splitting open like a popcorn kernel.

He lowered his gun and, as people started to peek out of the doorways and windows they had been hiding behind, walked leisurely down the street.

"That was fantastic!" Mort Suderson yelled, slapping the floor in front of the television. The film's end credits rolled across the screen as Nick Crecko, the Bloodmaster, disappeared into the sunset against the Los Angeles skyline. "Wasn't it great, Brett?"

"C'mon, Mort, it was crap," Macklin groaned, reaching toward the VCR atop the TV set.

"Wait! Don't turn it off yet. Don't you want to see our credit?" Mort looked at Macklin as if he were crazy. Macklin, raising his hands in a show of acquiescence, stepped back and watched the screen.

Aerial Transportation provided by: Blue Yonder Airways

"That's us!" Mort pointed at the set, wagging his finger excitedly. "That's us, boss! We're stars!"

Macklin clicked off the VCR and hit the eject button, tossing the videotape onto Mort's lap. "All we did was fly the film crew around. No one is going to nominate us for an Oscar."

Mort, reaching up and bracing himself on a couch cushion, rose to his feet and stretched. "Christ, Brett, I love hard-core police drama."

Macklin went into his kitchen, which adjoined the living room. "That was shit, Mort. C'mon, a fighter plane chasing a guy through downtown Los Angeles? Who are they kidding?"

Mort, glancing back to make sure he wasn't being watched, brushed potato chip crumbs off his faded blue jeans onto the shag carpet and then followed Macklin into the kitchen. "It's exciting. It isn't supposed to be Shakespeare."

Macklin opened the refrigerator. "What would you like, Mort?"

Mort eyed the six-pack of Schlitz longingly but knew better. Booze had already fucked up his life enough. "Gimme one of those Diet Cokes."

Macklin grabbed a beer for himself and handed Mort the diet drink. "I have a hard time separating what I know about the film makers from the film itself. Brock Dale, the guy who played macho Nick Crecko, is a whimpering homosexual, an egotistical little hemorrhoid in the ass of humanity."

"You've got to forget that." Mort snapped open the Diet Coke and took a big gulp. "On screen, he's the invincible Bloodmaster. Has been for years." Mort ambled into the living room and dropped himself onto Macklin's couch.

"Has-been is right." Macklin, sipping his beer, leaned against the kitchen doorway. He could hear raindrops tapping the roof. "But I have to admit, it was a nice way to kill a lazy, rainy afternoon."

"Yeah, I tell you, I'm going to fucking sue the Beach Boys," Mort said, pausing to swallow a mouthful of Diet Coke. "Did they ever mention week-long rainstorms in their songs, huh? No. The sun was always shining and everybody was getting laid. Do you see the sunshine? Do you see me getting laid?"

Mort shifted his gaze to the Duraflame log burning in the fireplace beside the TV. "But that's going to change."

"The weather or your sex life?" Macklin quipped.

"Who gives a shit about the weather? I can't do anything about that. I can fix my sex life. I'm going to make a few changes."

"Like what?"

"I'm thinking of changing my name," Mort offered cautiously. "I've thought it out and I think I'd make a good Mortimer *Neville*. It's sexy, it's now. It's a happening name. It's me."

Macklin stared silently at Mort.

"It's a great name, huh?" Mort continued, nervously filling the silence. "A real *fuckable* name. A guy with a name like that could get so much action he'd have to get his schlong insured against injury."

Mort stood up and started pacing in front of the fire. "Of course if I'm going to be that active with the ladies, I'm going to need an operation."

"Operation?" Macklin asked uneasily.

Mort stuck his tongue out, shoved his index finger under it, and approached Macklin. "I'm gonna have this little connection here snipped off," he slobbered. "It'll make my tongue longer. I think it's too short and I'm not adequately satisfying women with it, you know? I also plan to drop a few hundred bucks into some new clothes."

Their attention was drawn to the entry hall. The two men turned and saw a frowning Cheshire Davis, still in her white nurse's uniform, carrying two bags of groceries into the house. "That's disgusting, Mort, nauseating."

"How long have you been standing there?" Mort said, his face reddening.

She walked past Mort into the kitchen, her eyes scolding him. "Long enough, Mort."

Macklin started to laugh.

"Ah, fuck you, Brett," Mort shot back, reaching for his pseudosheepskin-lined Levi jacket lying in a heap on the floor. "It isn't funny. I was born handicapped, with a deformed tongue."

Macklin, rocking with laughter, spilled his beer on the floor. Cheshire, unpacking the groceries, began to laugh as well.

"It isn't funny!" Mort shouted. "I'm correcting a birth defect."

Realizing that he was making no headway with either of them, Mort gave up, stomping to the front door in a huff and yanking it open.

Macklin's laughter stopped abruptly. He saw Shaw standing in the doorway, his gray trenchcoat soaked with rain.

Mort looked over his shoulder at Brett for some kind of cue.

"See you later, Mort." Macklin caught his breath, his smile ebbing. Mort hesitated for a moment, uncertain whether to leave or not, then brushed past Shaw into the rain.

"Can I come in?" Shaw asked sheepishly.

Macklin looked over his shoulder at Cheshire, who was busy stuffing food into the refrigerator and apparently hadn't heard Shaw's voice. Macklin sighed, approaching Shaw quietly. He made no motion to invite him in.

"What is it?" Macklin demanded, careful to keep his voice low. He knew what Shaw wanted. Every morning Macklin awoke and wondered, *is this the day they come for me again?* The fear that his *wondering* might actually be *longing* kept him up nights.

"Mayor Stocker wants to see you," Shaw said.

Stocker wants you to pick up your gun again, a voice teased Macklin. *He wants you to dig it out from under the floorboards, slip the six bullets into the chamber, and squeeze the trigger. You'd like that, wouldn't you, Macky boy? You'd like that a lot.*

"No," Macklin said.

Shaw swallowed. "Look, Mack, you don't have any choice."

Macklin looked over his shoulder toward the kitchen. Cheshire was out of sight, probably putting food into the refrigerator. He faced Shaw again. "My life is becoming whole again. Do you want to shatter that?" He was asking the voice inside him. Not Shaw.

"No, I don't," Shaw replied, anger seeping defensively into his voice. "You know how I feel about it. But, it's not in my hands." Shaw immediately regretted the tone of his voice. None of the sympathy he actually felt came across.

To Shaw, Macklin's ocean-blue eyes suddenly dimmed, his face tightening into the savage look of determination that made Shaw doubt this was the same Brett Macklin he had grown up with. The look that symbolized the man Macklin had become since his father, a beat cop, was set aflame by a street gang. The look of a killer who made sure each of those gang members ended up in a burial plot.

It was that look, and the lawlessness it represented to Shaw, that made it impossible for Shaw to ever enjoy the deep friendship they once had.

"When does he want to see me?" Macklin's words seemed to have a serrated edge.

"Tomorrow morning. Nine o'clock."

"All right, I'll be there." Their eyes met for a second that felt like days to Shaw. He thought he saw a spark of vulnerability in Macklin's eyes and was about to say something, to reflexively grasp for their old closeness, when Macklin slowly closed the door in his face.

CHAPTER TWO

The punker with the tangerine-orange mohawk held a sawed-off shotgun, Macklin was sure of that. Macklin had seen him out of the corner of his eye as he drove past the Quick Stop market on his way to Stocker's office.

Macklin pressed the gas pedal to the floor. The black Cadillac shot forward. At the next intersection, Macklin twisted the wheel, whipping the car into a screeching U-turn and gliding it to a stop at the street corner a quarter block up from the market. He wasn't even thinking now. His anger was doing the thinking for him.

He didn't have his gun, but he wasn't going to let that stop him. The wooden skeleton of a building under construction adjoined the garage-sized Quick Stop market. Macklin assumed he could find a weapon at the construction site.

Macklin bolted out of the car and splashed through puddles on the sidewalk into the roofless structure beside the market. Crouching, Macklin searched the muddy concrete floor for a suitable weapon. He was about to settle for a damp two-by-four when he spotted a steel level lying amidst wood shavings and scattered nails. Picking it up, he swung it. The level was heavy in his hand. Yes. He smiled. This will do.

He slipped out the back of the structure into an alley and approached the market's back door. Cautiously, Macklin turned the doorknob with his left hand and slowly pushed the door open with his shoulder.

The door opened into a closet-sized storeroom lined with cardboard boxes. Macklin closed the door carefully behind him and could hear voices from just outside the storeroom's other door across from him.

"L-look, I-I don't have the combination to the safe, r-really," Macklin heard a young man plead in a voice made shrill with fear.

"Bullshit!" the punker rasped. "Open the fucking safe, or I'll blow your head off!" The punker sounded angry and impatient. Macklin thought it was only a matter of seconds before the punker lost his cool and the cashier would be splattered all over the room.

"*Open it!*" the punker shouted.

Macklin eased open the storeroom door and entered the market unseen. The market was bathed in flourescent white, three aisles running across the floor to the cashier, who was boxed in by counters cluttered with magazine displays and jars of candy. The punker, wearing snakeskin pants and a vest made of chains, shifted his weight in front of the counter, holding the shotgun six inches from the pimple-faced cashier's neck.

The cashier dumped a handful of change and crumpled bills onto the counter top in front of the punker.

"Here, that's all we have in the register," the boy stammered. "I don't know the combination to the safe, you have to believe me."

"You got two seconds to learn it, maggot," the punker barked.

Macklin stepped into the aisle behind the punker and crept forward, raising the level over his head. The cashier caught the movement behind the punker and, for an instant, stared right at Macklin.

Macklin frantically waved his hand, motioning the cashier to look away.

"Time's up, asshole, open it!" The punker jabbed the shotgun into the cashier's stomach. Macklin was two feet away.

"You're unbalanced, buddy," Macklin hissed.

The punker whirled around. Macklin swung the level at the punker's head like a baseball bat and felt the dull smack of steel against flesh. The punker fell, reflexively squeezing the trigger. The shotgun jerked, spitting fire. Macklin threw himself sideways into the candy rack, and the cashier screamed, leaping back against the Slurpee machine.

Macklin felt the shotgun pellets scorch past his right ear and heard them chew into the ceiling. Bits of plaster rained down like snowflakes.

Bracing himself against a shelf of Babe Ruth bars, Macklin rose carefully, deafened by the ringing echoes of the shotgun blast. Brushing plaster off his shoulders, he looked down at the twitching punker. Blood seeped out in frothy rivers from the left side of the punker's head, which now had the unnatural curve of a peanut shell.

Macklin shifted his gaze from the punker to the cashier, who cowered in shocked silence against the Slurpee machine. Cherry-colored ice fell out of the machine in huge glops.

"Are you okay?" Macklin asked, stepping up to the counter.

The boy nodded as if in a trance.

Macklin rested the level against his right shoulder and smiled reassuringly at the boy. "Why don't you stop leaning on the machine and come here for a second?"

The boy stared quizzically at Macklin for a moment and then suddenly realized his back was against the Slurpee lever. The boy jumped forward as if electrocuted, his back coated with red ice. A smile that shifted rapidly between embarrassment and relief filled his pimple-scarred face.

"Thanks. You, ah, saved my life."

"No problem," Macklin said. "Would you do me a favor?"

"Of course!" the cashier eagerly responded.

"When the police ask you what I look like, tell 'em I'm about five foot four, three hundred fifty pounds, and Oriental. Get my drift?"

The cashier looked confused. "S-sure. Anything."

Macklin smiled. "Thanks." He stepped toward the door and then stopped, returning to the counter. "Listen, could I have a large coffee?"

"Yeah, sure, a large coffee." The cashier spun around, grabbed for the coffee pot, and poured Macklin a cup. The coffee spilled out in a rush and flowed over the rim of the Styrofoam cup. The cashier didn't notice. He set the pot down and, forcing a broad smile, shakily handed Macklin the cup of coffee.

Macklin, the level in one hand and the coffee in the other, turned his back on the cashier, stepped over the punker, and strode to the door. "See you later. Thanks for the coffee."

"W-wait," the boy yelled as Macklin pushed open the front door with his shoulder. "Who are you?"

Macklin, his back to the cashier, smiled to himself. "The jury."

It was 9:45 when Macklin flung open Mayor Stocker's office door and sauntered in.

"I said nine o'clock, Macklin," Stocker barked, rising from behind his desk. Shaw, sitting on the vinyl couch against the wall to Stocker's right, groaned inside. The meeting was getting off to a *great* start.

Macklin shrugged. "I got held up.'

"Well, I don't give a shit." Stocker jerked a finger toward the two chairs fronting his desk. "Sit down, Macklin."

Macklin stayed where he was, in the center of the room, and shoved his hands deep into the pockets of his Levi 501s.

"Make it quick, Mayor." Macklin's words came out with measured evenness. It gave Shaw an unsettling chill.

Shaw glanced at Stocker, expecting an angry retort at Macklin's impudence, but none came. Stocker slid past the state flag and sat on the edge of his desk.

"Sergeant, tell Macklin our problem."

Macklin glanced at Shaw.

No, it's your problem, Stocker, Shaw thought, I can take care of this within the law. I don't want Macklin involved.

"Three little girls have been raped and strangled in the last month." Shaw looked at Stocker as he spoke, avoiding Macklin. Shaw felt if he directed his words to Macklin, he was somehow condoning the actions Macklin was going to be asked to take.

"Go on, Sergeant," Stocker prodded impatiently.

Shaw sighed, straightening up. "We know who's doing it," he continued reluctantly. "A psychopathic pedophile named Wesley Saputo. Five years ago, Saputo was in the kiddie porn film business. Backed by Crocker Orlock, a wealthy magazine distributor, Saputo made hundreds of low-low-budget films and then released them worldwide through a complex, underground pedophile network."

Shaw paused, glancing at Macklin to gauge his reaction. There was no change in the pilot's hard expression. "We were able to arrest Saputo and a couple of his cronies when his cameraman, a greasy character named Lyle Franken, was caught in an LAPD sting operation trying to sell kid porn photos. One of the photos was a blow-up from a Saputo film. It was a picture of a twelve-year-old girl who had recently been found raped and strangled."

Macklin turned to his left, his back to Shaw and Stocker, and stared out the window at the city's skyline. The buildings poked out through a thin layer of smog. Sunlight fought in vain to break through the noxious haze.

"Franken became a nonstop talker under pressure and we were able to send Saputo away on kiddie porn charges. We couldn't pin a thing on Orlock," Shaw said. "He managed to keep himself at arm's length from the operation. But he was behind it, no doubt about that."

Shaw paused, his feelings of frustration regarding the Saputo case stoked again by the retelling. He found himself getting caught up in the sort of anger that drove Macklin. The tension wrapped itself, boalike, around his neck, and squeezed. He fought against it, striving for cool detachment.

Shaw didn't want to feel like a part of what was going to take place in this office. "Saputo was labeled by the state shrinks as a mentally disordered sex offender, spent some time at Patton State Hospital, and then at Soledad. He was released on parole in September. The murders began in November."

"That's a fascinating story, gentlemen," Macklin said, his eyes scanning the city's steel peaks and asphalt valleys. "What does it have to do with me?"

"Kid porn has been nearly dead in this city for five years," Stocker replied. "Orlock had the money, but his talent was behind bars. Saputo is out now and Orlock isn't about to let his star film maker get caught again. Orlock's cadre of high-powered, Century City attorneys jumped on us and wrangled a court order that forbids us from harassing Saputo. We get within ten miles of him, and his lawyers drag us into court."

"Saputo has to be stopped before he kills again, Macklin," Stocker said evenly.

Macklin turned slowly to face Stocker. An amused smile played on Macklin's lips. "What you want me to do is kill him."

Shaw felt his stomach muscles tense up. He wanted to get up and walk out now, before he got in any deeper, but his body wouldn't move.

"No, we want you to *stop* him." Stocker's words came out as crisp and smooth as the stride of a man carrying a live bomb.

You mean kill, Shaw thought, you rotten son of a bitch. *And Mack will…*

"I won't be your executioner, Stocker. Then I'm as bad as the people you want me to ..." Macklin paused, a grin growing on his face "... the people you want me to stop."

Macklin paced in front of Stocker. "I think we need some due process here."

"What?" Stocker's eyebrows arched in angry disbelief.

"Saputo *could* be innocent." Macklin glanced at Shaw and was pleased to see the beginnings of a smile.

Some of the iciness Shaw felt toward Macklin was melting. Maybe this madness could end, Shaw thought. Maybe Mack is seeing that his way is wrong. Maybe ...

"Funny," Stocker said, walking toward Macklin, "you weren't exactly Mr. Due Process when you were avenging your father, were you? Saputo *is* guilty. We *both* know that. What's your problem, what more evidence do you need?"

"I'll gather the evidence I need while you and Shaw find someone, a judge or something, who can be our judicial review," Macklin said. "This third party can pass sentence. I want the judgment on whether to *stop* someone to come from him after a careful review of the evidence I gather. I want the decision called by someone besides you or me. I don't trust either one of us, Stocker."

Stocker laughed uproariously. "Macklin, you are out of your fucking mind. The answer is no. Period. You do as you're told."

Macklin smiled. "You don't give me orders. Suggestions perhaps, but not orders."

Stocker stepped within a foot of Macklin. "Are you forgetting I can have you arrested for multiple murders right this fucking second? You are in no position to tell *me* a damn thing!"

Macklin could smell the spearmint mouthwash on Stocker's breath. "You may be able to put me behind bars, but I can destroy you, the LAPD, and the whole city government," Macklin replied softly, undaunted by Stocker's rage.

"You're dreaming, Macklin."

Macklin pulled a cassette tape out of his pocket and tossed it to Shaw. "Play it," he demanded sharply, staring Stocker in the eye.

Okay, let's see what your game is, Mack, Shaw thought, sauntering casually across the room to Stocker's stereo system, popping in the cassette, and hitting the play button.

Static hummed over the speakers. Shaw heard a faint voice and turned the volume up.

"... so you've got problems in Chinatown." Macklin's voice was clearly recognizable over the speakers. "Big fucking deal. I still don't understand why you had Ron drag me down here."

"I told you about the problem in Chinatown because I want Mr. Jury to take care of it ..."

Stocker paled at the sound of his voice on the tape. Macklin's gaze remained fixed on Stocker's scowl-drawn face.

"Every conversation we had about the gang warfare I ended in Chinatown is on tape." Macklin said, obviously pleased with himself. "I walked in here wired."

"... these guys are no different than the men who killed your father. Go after them the same way. I'll make sure you get no heat from the police ..."

"Turn it off, Shaw," Stocker yelled.

Shaw didn't move. He wanted to see Stocker roast for a minute. Maybe if Stocker heard himself he'd see the lunacy. Maybe he'd understand. Maybe this crazy vigilante bullshit would end.

"... You're mine, Macklin. For better or worse, I own you."

"You never did, Stocker. And you never will." Macklin calmly walked over to the stereo and ejected the tape. "This is my version of mutual assured deterrence. You screw me and I'll screw you."

Macklin handed the tape to Stocker. "Keep this one as a souvenir."

The mayor grabbed the cassette and yanked out the tape, tearing it. He tossed the ruined cassette into the garbage can.

"Okay, you've both played your trump cards, now what?" Shaw spoke up, drawing their attention. It's time, Shaw thought, to inject some reality into this. "How do we find someone who can play God, decide who lives or dies? *What you're talking about is still murder.*"

Shaw let out a sigh of futility. "But you two have forgotten that, haven't you? All right, let's deal with this on a less philosophical plane. How do we find someone you and the mayor can both live with?"

Shaw walked in a broad circle around Stocker and Macklin. "What do we do, gentlemen? Approach someone and just say, 'Hello, we've got an assassin working for us. Would you mind playing referee'? Suppose we approach the wrong man and he goes to the *Los Angeles Times?*"

"You'll just have to find the right man, Ronny," Macklin said.

"I will?" Shaw half smiled. "Guess again."

Shaw was the one person under Stocker's influence whom Macklin could trust, the only person Macklin knew would look out for his interests as well as the LAPD's. "Ronny, revenge won't work as justification anymore."

"It never did, Mack." Shaw shook his head. "You're kidding yourself if you think anything will justify it now."

"Injustice, Ronny, that's our justification," Macklin replied. "The law isn't working. Too many criminals are going free and too many innocent people are getting hurt."

"Oh, spare me the ethical bullshit and let's get to the point, okay?" Stocker shuffled to his desk and fell into his seat. "We're talking about a fourth man. Someone else who knows, Macklin, that you're Mr. Jury."

"And knows you're encouraging me."

"What kind of man are we talking about?" Stocker ran his hands through his hair. Macklin had him by the balls. He had to show Macklin just how crazy the idea was. "A neo-conservative ex-judge like Sinclair Thompson, a lunatic liberal lawyer like

Frank Swift, or a mercurial, Harlan Fitz clone? Face it, Macklin, the three of us are in it alone. We are inextricably bound to each other."

"Harlan Fitz…" Macklin mused.

"A big-mouthed, headline-mongering ex-judge turned talk-show personality who has his head securely up his ass," Stocker snapped. Jesus, why can't Macklin understand? "The guy can't figure whether he's on our side or the ACLU's. He's a jackass. We both hate him. Case closed. We're back to square one."

"I've never heard of Harlan Fitz," Macklin mused, "but he sounds like our man. If both sides can't stand him, he must be doing something right."

Macklin walked toward the door. "Ronny, you approach him while I scope out Mr. Saputo."

Before either Stocker or Shaw could object, Macklin was gone.

CHAPTER THREE

There's no business like show business, it's like no business I know...

The needle was stuck on Brett Macklin's mental turntable. Ethel Merman belted out that lyric again and again in Macklin's head as he glided toward the red light at Overland and Culver Boulevard. He could understand why the song droned on. It was the toll charge the neighborhood exacted for driving through.

The MGM Studios water tower, with the logo of the company's latest film emblazoned on it, loomed a few blocks up under a blanket of bruised clouds. And to his right he saw the Veteran's Memorial Building fountain, frothy water gurgling through the sprockets of three intertwined steel strips fashioned like movie film.

This is movieland, he heard the neighborhood try to convince him, there is glitter here. You may not see it, but it's here.

The neighborhood merchants apparently saw it, somewhere behind the age-beaten Premiere Motel or beside Celebrity Hair Styling or around the corner from the Al's Star Burgers.

Macklin didn't see any. Maybe Wesley Saputo, riding in a tan four-door Seville two cars in front of him, did. The light switched to green and the traffic crawled eastward on the rain-slicked street toward downtown Culver City.

Macklin studied the buildings as he passed them. They looked like the facades pretending to be buildings on a Hollywood backlot. Cement and gray, art deco, fantasyland urbanity. If one could buy a business district at Ralph's, Macklin thought, this would be in the plain wrap section.

He sighed. He'd driven past here a thousand times and never cared about appearances before. Now he cared. Shit, he thought, am I bored. To drown out Ethel, he clicked on KROQ-FM and turned up the volume. A rebel yell from Billy Idol shook the car. Ethel sang on, undaunted.

Macklin had been following Saputo around for two days and had canceled several charter flights to find the time. He was beginning to get mad about all the money he had pissed away to play cops and robbers. Time Macklin could have spent in the air, flying charters and thereby paying the bills that cluttered his office, was killed in his car outside Saputo's apartment building listening to Dire Straits and Bruce Springsteen tapes.

At least Mort is flying, Macklin thought. It's a good thing, too, or I wouldn't have the money to pay him.

Macklin wouldn't have been upset if Saputo had at least done something incriminating. But Saputo rarely left his weed-land-scaped mustard-yellow Mar Vista apartment building except to run down to Safeway for groceries. Macklin was beginning to wonder if Stocker and Shaw knew what they were talking about.

Saputo turned right where Culver met Venice Boulevard and then veered left onto Robertson. Macklin followed, yawning, noticing with irritation that the afternoon was giving way to evening. The city was now enjoying the chilly afterglow of a day of cold, hazy blue sunshine.

The Seville wound through a mazelike path of side streets lined with bland, boxy one-and two-story industrial buildings before pulling over beside a windowless warehouse. Macklin drove past the warehouse, made a U-turn two blocks away, and came back. He stopped behind a cement mixing truck parked kitty-corner from the warehouse and turned off his ignition.

He watched Saputo rise from the passenger side of the Seville. Three hairless grizzly bears stuffed into camel-colored slacks and

Sanka-brown corduroy jackets emerged from the car after him. Macklin had no doubt the three apes packed some heavy artillery under those carved-granite shoulders.

Macklin studied Saputo, who strutted toward the warehouse door in his Jordache jeans, tan polyester jacket, and red silky dress shirt unbuttoned down to the bulge of his stomach. A gold chain tapped against his bony chest with each footfall.

It was Macklin's first real opportunity to look at the man. In the next brief second or two, Macklin knew Stocker and Shaw were right. He saw it in Saputo's self-impressed gait, in the narrow I'm-fucking-your-wife-and-your-daughter-too grin, in the eyes that conveyed a schoolyard bully's childish defiance and disrespect.

Macklin saw Saputo slip a key into the steel door, which was the bottom right corner of a much larger door that could slide up to let in trucks. Saputo stepped inside, two guards galloping after him like pet dogs. The third man stayed outside grimacing, apparently unhappy at having to perform sentry duty.

Macklin settled back in his seat, pushed a Doors tape in the Sanyo, and prepared for a long wait. The guard lit a cigarette, reached down with one hand to adjust his balls, and began to pace in front of the warehouse, blowing smoke out of his mouth in tiny circles.

A van wound around the corner in front of Macklin, the headlight beams cutting a swath in the darkness toward his head. Macklin ducked down as the light passed through the car and glanced at his watch. It was 8:04 P.M. Roughly three hours had passed since he had parked outside the warehouse.

Macklin sat up and saw the van pull up to the warehouse door. The driver honked twice. The sentry, facing Macklin's direction as he appeared around the edge of the warehouse, tossed away a glowing cigarette butt and walked around the back of the van to the driver's side.

The driver and the sentry knew each other, Macklin assumed, because the sentry stayed there chatting as the steel warehouse door rose noisily. Bright light spilled from inside the warehouse and bathed the van in whiteness. The van surged forward, and Macklin could see the end of a laugh on the sentry's face. The warehouse door dropped quickly, swallowing the van and the light. But not before Macklin caught a glimpse of the van's license plate.

Macklin scribbled the plate number down on a notepad beside him, adding to the list of plate numbers he had copied from cars parked around the warehouse.

The sentry walked toward Macklin without noticing him and then turned around the edge of the warehouse, disappearing from Macklin's view.

Macklin scratched his cheek. Hmmm.

His buttocks ached, and he was sick of listening to his tapes. And nothing was happening outside the warehouse. All the action was inside. Macklin figured those were good reasons to get up, stretch, and give the warehouse a careful look-over.

He opened the door, stepped outside, and bent over, touching his toes. His back cracked audibly. Macklin frowned. *I'm turning into a fat old man.* Lately, Macklin had come to accept he wasn't the muscular youth who had dashed through UCLA on a track scholarship anymore.

Macklin closed the door, careful to muffle the sound, and sprinted stealthily across the street to the shadows of the office building beside the warehouse. By now the sentry is directly behind Saputo's warehouse, Macklin thought. If I'm alert, I can circle the building undetected and stay behind the sentry.

Abandoning his cover in the shadows against the building, he dashed lightly on the balls of his feet across the alley to the side of Saputo's warehouse. As he moved along the wall, he noticed the cement expanse had no doors or windows.

Macklin slid his body around the back of the warehouse and saw the back of the sentry disappearing around the opposite side.

This wall, too, had no openings. He sprinted across the length of the warehouse and paused before rounding the next corner. Peering around the wall's edge, he saw the sentry standing next to a garbage bin. The sentry struck a match on the edge of the bin, his fleshy face momentarily illuminated as he lit the cigarette that dangled between his puffy lips.

The sentry flicked his smoking match away and shuffled along the asphalt to the front of the warehouse. As soon as the sentry rounded the corner, Macklin crept quietly over to the trashbin. He noticed that a rust-coated padlock clamped the bin closed.

What kind of trash is so important that you lock it up? Macklin wondered, tugging on the padlock. He stared at the bin, letting his imagination assume the worst. In his mind, he could see his nine-year-old daughter, Corinne, amidst the trash, neck sliced open, maggots squirming over her bloated, decaying face.

He shivered, his stomach churning.

You've got a sick mind, Mack, a real sick mind.

Macklin dashed back, the way he had come, to the rear of the warehouse and crossed the alley to the rear of the adjacent office building. He went around the side of the building and paused, glancing to his left to see where the sentry was. The sentry was out of sight, probably beginning his circle around the warehouse again. Macklin trotted to his car and got inside.

He took a deep breath and studied the warehouse. *What are you doing in there, Wesley?* Macklin reached out to the glovebox with his right hand. Sitting beside the .357 Magnum was a Baggie full of cut carrots. He pulled out the bag, closed the glovebox, and clicked on the stereo. Munching on his carrots, he scrunched down in his seat and waited, letting his mind wander to thoughts of Cheshire.

He was glad Cheshire had the night shift this week and wouldn't be stumbling into the house until after midnight. She'd be less aware of his absence and would be less likely to question his excuses.

Cheshire was spending four to five nights a week at Macklin's Venice home. Macklin remembered how uncomfortable it had felt at first, how scared and pressured her presence had made him feel. But those uncomfortable feelings ebbed with surprising speed and were replaced by an urgency, a need to spend time with her.

Macklin found it all so ironic. Becoming involved with her had never been part of his plans. They had met nearly a year ago, during the horrible weeks after his father's murder.

She had gone to nursing school with Mort's sister and had patched up the stab wound Macklin received in a deadly struggle with one of the gang members who had killed his father.

He used her then, making love to her and spending the night with her as an alibi. While she slept, Macklin snuck away to kill one of the murderers.

But after his father had been avenged, Macklin continued to see her. In fact, she was the only person he saw. He couldn't bring himself to see his daughter, Cory, or Brooke, his ex-wife. Not after what he had done. Not after what he had become.

Cheshire was part of his new life. Cory and Brooke were part of his old life, a life sacrificed to the driving compulsion inside him that the public called Mr. Jury. For now, despite his love for Cory, Cheshire was all he had.

He felt that being with Cheshire was rebuilding him. He was beginning to feel that he might be able to recapture some of what he had lost.

The small warehouse door opened, interrupting Macklin's introspection. Wesley Saputo, accompanied by his two guards, emerged from inside and sauntered to the Seville. Saputo was hyped up, talking excitedly, his hands moving quickly to illustrate some point. They waited for the sentry to join them, and then the four men got into the Seville. The headlights flashed on and the engine roared to life.

Macklin ducked down as the Seville sped past him. When the car had turned the corner, Macklin started up his car and drove to the edge of the warehouse, stopping next to the trashbin. Leaving the engine running, he got out and opened the trunk.

He pulled out a pair of bolt cutters and a Glad trash bag and closed the trunk. His face etched with determination, Macklin pinched the padlock between the cutting blades and snapped the clasp. Dropping the bolt cutters, he lifted open the trashbin.

The sour stench of decay smacked him, curling his face into a wince. *God, what a smell.* Macklin, breathing through his mouth to avoid the smell, leaned into the bin, searching through the rotten food, empty bottles, and cans. He grabbed handfuls of damp, slippery paper and three typewriter ribbon cartridges and shoved them into the bag.

Closing the bin, he picked up the bag and his bolt cutters and returned to the car. Macklin turned on his interior light and examined the contents of the bag.

A wave of nausea rocked Macklin as he gazed at three soiled, torn, and yellowed photos of naked girls, no older than ten or eleven, being fondled by men with hungry grins.

The bastards…

He shoved the photos back into the bag. I'm going to stop this shit, Macklin thought. What Saputo is doing is inhuman. Macklin flipped off the interior light, started the engine, and drove away.

Had Macklin looked in his rear-view mirror, he would have seen the dark form standing at the edge of the warehouse behind him, watching.

The thin man turned and walked casually to a coal-black BMW, parked in the shadows across from the warehouse. In what seemed like one fluid, choreographed motion, he opened the door, sat down, and reached for the telephone between the seats.

"Mr. Orlock?" The man's words slithered out snakelike—soft and smooth. "This is Tice."

"Good evening, Tice," Orlock replied lightly.

"The stranger followed Wesley to the warehouse and just broke into our trash."

"Really?" Orlock laughed. "Our trash, huh? We can't have that, Tice, now can we?"

"No, sir," Tice whispered.

"A man's trash is sacred."

"Yes, sir." Tice smiled thinly.

"You'd better kill the fiend."

"As you wish." Tice clicked off the phone.

CHAPTER FOUR

Cheshire was curled up in the corner of the couch in her yellow terrycloth bathrobe watching *Late Night with David Letterman* when Macklin came in the front door carrying a small grocery bag.

"Mack, I thought you'd never get back," Cheshire said as he rushed past her into the kitchen.

"I'm sorry, there was more office work at the hangar than I thought." Macklin set the bag down on the kitchen table. "But I got you a little surprise to make up for it."

Cheshire rose from the couch, turned off the television, and trudged barefoot into the kitchen. "What?"

Macklin melodramatically yanked a quart of chocolate ice cream from the grocery bag. "Ta da!"

Cheshire laughed. "I appreciate it, honey, but it's too fattening."

Macklin frowned. "Fattening? Cheshire, are you going to deny yourself one of life's greatest pleasures?"

"Yep."

"Okay." Macklin shrugged, turning his back to Cheshire and reaching toward the kitchen cabinets above the sink for a bowl.

"Forget the bowls, Brett," Cheshire said. He turned around and saw her holding two spoons in one hand and yanking open the quart with the other. "Half the fun is just digging in. It doesn't give you time to think about the calories."

He grinned, shaking his head disbelievingly, and took a spoon from her, plunged it into the ice cream, dug out a huge portion, and eagerly stuffed it into his mouth.

"Good?" she asked with an expectant smile.

"*Great.*" He pointed to the ice cream with his spoon as if she needed urging on.

"I'm going to savor this," she said, wagging her spoon at him.

"Okay already, so eat."

Cheshire stabbed the ice cream with her spoon, carved out a thick wedge, and sucked the end of it into her mouth. She closed her eyes and rolled the ice cream between her cheeks. "Mmmmmmmm," she purred.

"Good?" Macklin asked.

She opened her eyes and nodded, the motion tipping her spoon. The remaining ice cream in her spoon spilled off inside her bathrobe.

Cheshire shrieked, dropping the spoon on the table.

"Shit!" she snapped, quickly untying her bathrobe.

Macklin saw the ice cream roll between her breasts, the chill raising goosebumps on her tan flesh and drawing her nipples into sharp points. He took her hand as she reached back for a towel.

He looked into her hazel eyes, stuck his free hand into the ice cream container, and clawed out a handful of chocolate. She tilted her head to one side and regarded him quizzically. Smiling, he smeared it deliberately over her left breast. She tossed her head back and gritted her teeth, drawing in a fast, deep breath.

Macklin's heart raced as he massaged a handful of ice cream over her other breast. Rivers of chocolate ran down her stomach and onto her panties. Leaning over, Macklin began to lick the ice cream off her breasts while one chocolate-covered hand massaged the warmth between her legs.

Cheshire moaned deeply, her nipples hard, pulsating points of chilly pleasure. Her icy ecstasy was invigorating, overpowering. She tore open his shirt, reached behind him, and plunged her hands into the carton, grabbing two handfuls of ice cream and rubbing it onto his back.

Macklin arched his back in reaction to the cold, pressing his wet, sticky lips into her neck and his hips against hers. She took his face into her hands and kissed him, her fingers entwined in his hair. Macklin eased down her panties, filled his hands with ice cream, and pressed the chocolate between her legs. She gasped in shock and pleasure, her mouth open in a wide smile.

"Goddamn, Brett Macklin!" she cried, her breaths coming hard and fast. She growled playfully, unbuckled his belt, and yanked down his pants. His erection strained against his bikini briefs. She took a handful of ice cream with one hand and pulled down the briefs with the other.

Macklin laughed. "Cheshire…"

"Yes?" She giggled mischievously and then wrapped her ice cream-filled hand around his stiff penis. Macklin choked back a scream. Cheshire laughed, dropped to her knees, and ran her tongue slowly up the shaft of his penis.

Macklin moaned and fingerpainted her back with chocolate fingers. He'd never felt so hard.

She reached for more ice cream, knocking over the empty container. Macklin clasped Cheshire by the shoulders, pulled her up, and kissed her, wrapping his arms around her and drawing her tight against him. Pushing her back against the kitchen counter, he entered her. She wrapped her legs around his waist, her hands grabbing his ass.

They moved against each other slowly at first, but their eagerness took over and soon they were undulating quickly, sharply, streams of melting chocolate ice cream streaming down their heaving bodies.

They let out surprised, muffled shrieks as they came, shivering with chills of cold and pleasure.

Macklin tried to catch his breath, his cheek against Cheshire's breast. He could feel her heart pulsing. "Now that's what I call a chocolate sundae." He grinned.

Cheshire threw back her head in a wild, satisfied laugh. "I love you, Brett, you sneaky little shit, I really do."

Macklin closed his eyes and felt something stiffen defensively inside him. He had the momentary impulse to walk away from her. Defying the urge, he suddenly lifted her up into his arms. She shrieked playfully. Laughing, with more gaiety than he felt, he carried her upstairs to his bedroom, where they showered, dried each other off, and made love again under the heavy comforter. They drifted off to sleep, snug in the warmth afforded by each other's arms.

Cheshire woke up at 6 A.M., ravenously hungry, yearning for a big country breakfast. She slipped out of bed carefully, trying not to wake up Brett, and crept naked down the stairs into the kitchen.

She paused in the doorway to the kitchen and surveyed the mess, hugging herself and feeling goosebumps on her shoulders. The empty ice cream container lay on its side on the kitchen table. Dried rivers of melted ice cream ran down the wood cabinets and settled on the floor in brownish puddles. It looked like the aftermath of a precocious child's fun or a wild raccoon's scavenging.

She frowned, knowing Brett would find a way around helping to clean up the mess, and stepped toward the refrigerator. The cold floor shattered whatever remnants of sleep remained. She tiptoed hurriedly across the floor as if she were walking barefoot on an ice rink.

Shivering, she hunched in front of the refrigerator and pulled it open. A wave of cold air splashed against her and the bright light from inside stung her eyes.

OhhhhhI' mmmmmsoooooocccccccooooldddd!

Being cold didn't feel so bad last night, did it?

Cheshire grinned nastily. *No, it didn't.* She peered into the refrigerator. She frowned again. The refrigerator looked like some kind of icy mausoleum. There were dozens of tiny aluminum-and plastic-wrapped bundles of indiscernible food lining the shelves like so many corpses. No eggs. No milk. No margarine.

If she wanted a country breakfast, she realized, it would have to be frozen pizza, left-over chicken, Schlitz beer, and some stale Grape Nuts cereal. *Damn!* She wanted to surprise Brett with a big, rousing breakfast.

No, be honest. You just wanted to be a pig!

She closed the refrigerator and bounced on her feet, trying to stay warm while she considered her options. Cheshire wasn't about to let the sorry selection in the refrigerator ruin her plans.

Nope, she was going to have her country breakfast. At home. In bed. Maybe, she thought, we can even play around a bit before I have to get my butt in gear and head to the hospital.

Safeway is just three blocks away, she reminded herself. Throw something on. Brett's sleeping like a baby. It will take a few sticks of dynamite to wake Brett up. Hurry. You can still have your country breakfast.

Cheshire dashed up the stairs, slipped into a pair of faded jeans and a loose-fitting, white sweatshirt, tucked her feet into a pair of sandals, and stole Brett's car keys and a few bucks off the dresser. She was down the stairs and out the door in twenty seconds.

The crisp, cold air slapped her as she dashed across the porch and through the front lawn, soaking her feet on the wet grass as she ran to the driveway between the rusted, decrepit Cadillacs that languished in the yard until Brett found the spare time to restore them.

Half-frozen beads of dew gave the black Cadillac in the driveway the icy look of an Eskimo Pie. Cheshire, anxious to get warm, quickly unlocked the door and got in. She slid the heater control to high. Cheshire wanted a warm blast as soon as possible.

She pumped the gas pedal, slipped the key into the ignition, and turned it.

The fiery explosion sent a hot wind crashing through Brett Macklin's bedroom window. Instinct tossed Macklin off the bed in the turbulent split second when the hellish roar rocked the house and blew a windstorm of glass shards sweeping through the room. Macklin, confused and twisted amidst the sheets on the floor, thought it was an earthquake.

He blinked open his eyes and sat up, still groggy from sleep and dazed by the sudden shudder that had tossed him out of bed. His thoughts, like the bedroom, were in utter disarray. Macklin propped himself up on the bed and, facing the window, saw the heavy brown smoke spiraling upward outside and smelled something burning.

What the fuck happened?

Macklin ran to the window, oblivious to the broken glass slicing his feet, and looked down.

He saw a car door, charred and smoldering on the steaming lawn.

Cheshire...

Macklin whipped his head around. Cheshire wasn't in the room. Naked, he frantically bolted out of the room and raced down the stairs, flinging open the front door and jumping off the porch onto the grass. Rounding the corner of the house, he felt the burning heat of the blaze before he saw the bright yellow flames eating out the inside of the Batmobile.

Macklin ran toward the car, but was pushed back by the searing heat. He could see the ravenous flames chewing into the vague, smoky outline of a person in the front seat.

He tried to scream her name, but his overwhelming feeling of hopeless frustration stole his breath. His lungs were being strangled by something strong and cold, something he had felt before, only months ago.

Macklin closed his eyes and fell to his knees.

Forgive me, Cheshire, forgive me...

CHAPTER FIVE

Shaw had a sickly feeling of *déjà vu* as he stood watching the firefighters douse the smoking, gnarled remains of the Cadillac.

He relived a warm, still night in a poverty-stricken south-central Los Angeles neighborhood. The black detective remembered the gutted, smoldering remains of the RTD bus, the body bags in the street, the unrecognizable charred lump of sizzling flesh that had once been LAPD Officer J. D. Macklin.

The RTD bus had wound around the corner when Brett's father ran aflame across its path. The bus driver swerved to miss him. The bus roared into oncoming traffic, smashing into cars and bursting into flames that nearly reduced an entire city block to smoldering ash.

Brett Macklin had seen those flames, too. And from them, Mr. Jury was born.

Shaw, grimacing, turned away from the firefighters and approached Macklin, who sat on the porch steps in his maroon wool bathrobe. Macklin stared coldly with glazed eyes at the wall of pajama-clad neighbors gawking at him on the sidewalk and listened to the steady streams of soot-blackened water rushing down the driveway and splashing into the gutter.

"Mack?" Shaw ventured softly. Macklin showed no sign of having heard him.

"Mack?" he repeated, shaking Macklin's shoulder. "Are you okay?"

Macklin's head shot up. "Am I okay? What kind of goddamn question is that?" His anger flared, lighting his eyes with rage and shattering his shocked lethargy. "Sure, Ronny, I'm just great. My lover was blown to bits in my driveway this morning. Am I okay? Sure, I've never felt better."

Macklin stood up, pushed Shaw roughly aside, and stormed toward the front door of the house.

Shaw made a move to follow him and Macklin whirled around, lashing out and striking Shaw in the chest with the palm of his hand.

"A year ago my life was ripped apart by a bunch of savages," Macklin yelled. "They set my father on *fire*, they poured gasoline on him and watched him *burn*. When they tossed that match on my father, they also set fire to my life." Macklin nodded toward the driveway. "I was beginning to think maybe, just maybe, I could become a normal human being again. Fuck, those savages won't let me."

Macklin, his face flushed with anger, poked Shaw hard in the chest with an accusing finger. "*You* won't let me."

Mackling yanked open the front door and slammed it shut behind him. Shaw sighed and stared at the closed door, torn between leaving and going inside. An old feeling, one of friendship and need, drew him toward the door while a strong, new feeling of distance and repulsion pulled him away.

"Shit," Shaw muttered to himself. "I hate this job."

Shaw cautiously eased open the door and peered into the house. Macklin, pacing back and forth in the living room, froze for an instant when he saw Shaw and leveled a gaze ripe with violence at the black detective.

Shaw entered the house anyway, eyeing Macklin with the wary attention of a man who accidentally crosses a lion's path in the jungle. Shaw closed the door softly behind him and took a tentative step into the entry hall.

Macklin turned away and continued pacing, ignoring him. Shaw slipped his hands into his pants pockets and remained standing in place, feeling awkward and claustrophobic.

"I can't face my daughter anymore, not after what I've done." Macklin kept pacing, his gaze cast to the floor. Shaw could barely hear him. "I'm afraid the blood on my hands will smear her, that the horror will take her like it's taken everyone I've touched since Dad was killed. I love her more than anything in this world, and I can't hold her.

"It's a disease, a fucking disease!" Macklin yelled suddenly, startling Shaw. Macklin ripped a framed print from the wall over the mantelpiece and swung it like a bat against the opposite wall again and again, until he had shattered it to bits.

"Don't you see? The same disease that took my father is infecting me." Macklin advanced angrily on Shaw and grabbed him by the neck with both hands. Shaw fought to stay calm. "It eats away at me late at night. It pokes and prods me until I break out in a cold sweat and grit my teeth to hold back the screams."

Macklin shook him. "*I want to kill!* I want to cut these savages away like a tumor. Do you understand? There's a side of me that wants pure carnage and, goddamnit, you're feeding that. You and Stocker and the slime on the streets—you're pushing me into it, begging me to do it. I can't help myself. I want to even the scales, make it right again. I *need* to make it right again."

Macklin stared into Shaw's eyes and saw himself. Macklin saw his wild eyes, his sweat-dampened face, his cheeks red with fury, his jaw tight with rage.

Make them pay.

For the first time, Macklin saw the face behind the voice that had driven him to kill. The voice that was urging him to kill again.

Make them pay.

Macklin gently released Shaw and saw the reddish impressions his fingers left on Shaw's throat. Macklin took two steps back and held up his hands in a show of surrender.

Shaw hoarsely cleared his throat and took a deep breath, his hands still in his pockets.

"Last night she said she loved me," Macklin whispered. "For a minute I thought I could have it all again. Happiness. Peace. Someone to love. And in a split second it's gone. Up in flames. I can almost hear someone laughing at me."

Macklin stepped up to Shaw again and gently rested his hands on Shaw's shoulders. "I'm sorry, Ronny. It's just that...I don't want to lose anyone else. I know you can't accept who and what I am now. But try. This time you came to me, this time you *asked* me to do it. You're part of what I've become."

He drew Shaw close into a tight embrace. Shaw felt stiff, uninvolved, as if he were watching it all on television, but he wrapped his arms around Macklin anyway.

"I'll try to be a friend to you," Shaw whispered raspily. "But what you're doing is wrong. It's against everything I believe, everything your father believed. I can't turn my back to that."

Macklin leaned away from Shaw. "Ronny, you and I grew up together. We are brothers."

"That's what makes it so hard." Shaw shrugged off Macklin's arms and turned toward the door. "Remember what you said to Mayor Stocker about law and order, judicial review. Don't betray yourself by picking up a gun and playing vigilante again."

Shaw opened the door, stepped outside, and paused for a moment, his back to Macklin. Sunlight bathed Shaw and cast his shadow on Macklin.

"I'm sorry about Cheshire," Shaw said. "I want the people who did this as badly as you do." He pulled the door closed, shutting out the sunlight and leaving Macklin alone in the dim, smoky living room.

"No," Macklin said to the closed door. "No you don't."

"Judge For Yourself!" the toothsome host yelled, a huge grin stretched across his face. "The show that puts *you* behind the bench and sentences you to prizes like ... A BRAND NEW CAR!"

The studio shuddered with shrieks of glee and hundreds of clapping hands. The clatter sounded to Shaw, standing behind the window of the control booth to the rear of the audience, like a flock of deranged birds.

The stage curtain behind the host opened. Lights flashed. Buzzers rang. A buxom brunette drove a glossy silver Oldsmobile Cutlass across the stage, parking it in front of the massive judge's bench that dominated the set.

The cameras panned over the audience, zooming in on the clapping, cheering, screaming, hysterically happy women bobbing in their seats. The show's synthesizer-born theme song blared over the speakers beside the flashing APPLAUSE signs above the stage.

The host swept his hand over the set behind him. "Now, meet our two contestants!" Two smaller judges' benches, one occupied by a woman with an overbite and the other by a black marine, appeared on either side of the set as if under the host's magical control.

Shaw shifted his weight uncomfortably. He didn't like being here. The emotional echo of his heated encounter with Macklin this morning was strong. Now here he was watching *this*. The contrast made him slightly dizzy. Or perhaps it was just the claustrophobic control room, the heavy cloud of cigarette smoke, the dreamlike glitz and blitz of the game show.

Or Shaw's fear. Coming here could be, he realized, the biggest mistake of his life.

"Okay, two, zoom in on Dirk," the director said into mouthpiece of his headset in a voice that sounded like it escaped from a throat filled with splintered wood. The camera-two TV monitor filled with the host's face.

"...just predict the judge's verdict on these real, small-claims cases and you win!" The perpetually grinning host sauntered behind his podium on the far side of the set. "And now, here's our judge, the Honorable Harlan Fitz!"

"Camera three, close on Fitz, cue the commercial," the direction mumbled perfunctorily. These same shots, Shaw assumed, were called day in and day out.

Harlan Fitz appeared at the bench, in his traditional judge's attire, with what Shaw thought to be a tired grimace on his face. Fitz was a broad-shouldered, strong fifty-five-year-old man, and his face had aged well. Shaw noticed it hadn't fattened or sagged with time. A gray-brown moustache and beard gave him a scholarly look. Age only showed itself in the few lines across his brow, the puffy bags emerging under his eyes, and the slight recession of his hairline.

The *Judge for Yourself* theme music swelled as Fitz took his seat, and the audience clapped like performing seals ready to do tricks.

The host pointed at the camera. "Stay right there, the excitement begins right after this!"

"Okay, bring up the music, camera one pull back wide." The director raised his hand, his index finger extended. "Aaaaaand," he whipped his arm down and jabbed the woman beside him "roll commercial."

The commercial filled the screen. A good-looking woman, apparently a lawyer, ran through the courtroom, breezed through an executive board meeting, and whisked past the maître d' of a fine restaurant to a table.

"Gee, Mary, how do you stay so active?" her plain-looking harried female lunch companion asked, her voice dripping with absolute awe.

Mary reached into her purse. *"New You*-brand tampons!"

Shaw sighed, switching his attention from the monitor to the stage. Technicians scurried on the set like ants. Fitz sat stoically at his bench, staring blankly into the audience. Shaw felt a little sad. This wasn't the Harlan Fitz who had once been a feared judge and outspoken critic of the inadequacies of the law.

Shaw thought back to the Public Disorder Intelligence Division file on Fitz he had read after the meeting with Macklin in Stocker's office several days ago. The report attributed Fitz's retirement to political and personal pressures. It concluded that Fitz was overwhelmed by the futility of battling what he saw as the inadequacy of the law and became disheartened by the lack of cooperation from fellow judges. Exasperated and exhausted, he retired.

Fitz became a nomadic media personality, a frequent guest on radio and TV programs. According to the numerous newspaper clippings of interviews done with Fitz that Shaw read in the PDID file, Fitz thought he could educate the public, initiate change. The media exploited Fitz's outrage, Shaw believed, ignoring the man's insights and turning his vehement attacks on the legal system into entertainment.

Shaw studied Fitz now as the director signaled the cameramen that the commercial break was nearly over. Shaw thought Fitz looked lost. He prayed to God that he was reading Fitz right. That assumption was his long-shot. Macklin, the city for that matter, depended on that.

Yet once the commercial was over, Shaw watched Fitz come alive, whittling away what little confidence Shaw had in his all-important assumption.

Fitz played the game with wit and vigor, appearing both knowledgeable and authoritative. Even interested. That was no small feat. The contestants were argumentative morons with no concept of the law or, it seemed to Shaw, simple logic.

Once the next commercial break came, Shaw noticed the judge sag, the glow disappearing from his face. Unlike the toothy host, when the cameras went off, so did Fitz.

Maybe, Shaw thought, just maybe there is some hope.

After a few more cases were heard, Ms. Overbite broke the 0 to 0 deadlock with the black marine and won the game. Then came the "judge-off" for the car. She had to match Fitz's decision on a particular case. Shaw didn't hear the host read the question, but it had something to with premature ejaculation, mud wrestling, break dancing, and a set of broken skis.

Ms. Overbite closed her eyes and clutched the host. Her lip quivering, she announced her decision. She looked hopefully at Fitz. A prerecorded drum rolled. A hush fell on the audience. Fitz held up a gavel-shaped placard with his answer scrawled across in felt-tipped marker. Their decisions matched.

The woman screamed joyfully, jumping around the host like a hysterical kangaroo. As the audience went wild with applause, Shaw slipped out of the control room and into a narrow slate-gray corridor. He shuffled toward a door a dozen footsteps away. Harlan Fitz's name, hastily handwritten in capital letters on a sheet of typing paper, was affixed to the door with yellow masking tape. As Shaw neared Fitz's door, his fear grew. He knew that Fitz had frequently—and publicly—chastised the ill-prepared prosecutors, careless cops, and sleazy lawyers who let criminals slip through the justice system unscathed. That's what had gotten the PDID interested in him. But Shaw also knew his proposal could just piss off Fitz even more. The judge could go to the press.

And then comes the end of the world.

Shaw turned the doorknob and stepped inside. He immediately felt cramped for breathing space. The windowless room seemed to him to be barely larger than his car. The lack of circulation gave the room the hot, oppressive quality of a hot oven recently used to cook a batch of Arrid Extra Dry. A white wood table and light bulb-lined mirror claimed half the room, and two folding chairs were propped against the opposite wall.

He opened a chair and sat down, crossed his legs, and waited.

It will work out, Ronny.

Shaw laughed to himself. *Yeah, sure.*

He heard footsteps outside, and before he could brace himself, Fitz pushed open the door.

"I see you found my dressing room, Sergeant." Fitz grinned, dropping heavily into the folding chair opposite Shaw. Gone were the judge's robes. Fitz was in the sweat-dampened shirt and jeans he had worn under his robes, which he had rolled up into a ball and placed on his dressing table.

"What did you think of the show?" Fitz asked, slapping Shaw's knee.

"It was very entertaining," Shaw replied.

Fitz laughed. "Bullshit."

Shaw smiled awkwardly, not knowing whether to join in Fitz's laughter.

"You probably hated it more than I did," Fitz said. "Look, a guy has to make money. Maybe I'm educating someone out there, who knows?"

"Well, it educated me, if that means anything," Shaw replied. "It's the first time I've even been behind the scenes, so to speak, of a TV show. I'm impressed."

"Thank you. You're very kind, Sergeant." Fitz's smile waned. "So why exactly do you want to talk with me?"

Shaw shifted uneasily in his seat. "Well, that isn't easy." He dropped his gaze and pondered his feet. Unable to think of an easy way to approach it, Shaw opted for the bottom line. "What do you know about Mr. Jury?"

"I know he's a vigilante who has killed half a dozen people."

"That's all?" Shaw asked, chancing to look at Fitz. The judge frowned.

"What more do you want, Sergeant? The guy is running around doing what most of us would like to do."

"Would you call it a sort of justifiable homicide?" The remark didn't come from Shaw but the script Shaw chose to perform. It was as if he was part of an undercover operation, playing a role. Nothing, to him, could ever be said to justify Macklin's actions.

"Just what are you getting at, Sergeant? I just got done playing the only game I want to for today." Fitz folded his arms across his chest and pinned Shaw under a stern gaze.

"What if I were to tell you Mr. Jury is interested in introducing some due process into his vigilante justice?"

"I'd say it's still vigilante justice," Fitz replied. He stared into Shaw's eyes, trying to see something there. Shaw wanted to get up and run.

"And I'd say it seems Mr. Jury is a better man than I thought," Fitz said slowly. His eyes narrowed. "Am I talking to Mr. Jury?"

"No," Shaw responded quickly. Too quickly, he thought.

"All right, Sergeant," Harlan Fitz groaned testily. "Let's quit the sparring. Make your point."

"What would you say if Mr. Jury wanted you to be that due process, to evaluate evidence and determine who, within the scope of the law, is guilty or innocent?" Shaw's throat felt raw, stone dry.

Fitz's stare didn't waver. The silence in the room was a crushing weight on Shaw's shoulders that grew heavier with each hourlong moment.

"I'd say my phone number is in the book."

CHAPTER SIX

That next afternoon mother nature got angry. She blew the rainclouds away with fierce gale-force winds that blasted through the city, ripping trees out of the ground, tearing off roofs, severing powerlines, and smashing in plate-glass windows.

People on the street, who were still recovering from five days of pounding rain, were caught by surprise and were tossed around like leaves by their wind-opened umbrellas. Tourists must have thought they were watching a sadistic *Mary Poppins* sequel in the making.

The merciless weather, along with a merciless editor, kept Jessica Mordente away from her desk at the *Los Angeles Times* and out on the street for most of the day. Her Thomas Brothers street map was her bible as she raced around the city interviewing the victims of mother nature's wrath.

She talked to an irate starlet in Beverly Hills whose pink Rolls Royce was crushed by a tree. Then Mordente sped west to the Santa Monica pier, where the wind had kicked one of the city's notorious vagrants into the sea. After two more hours of on-the-spot reporting, Mordente shoved her three full reporter's notebooks into her purse and headed downtown for the *Times* building.

Mordente remained in front of her computer terminal for the rest of the afternoon piecing together a story from her notes and frequent telephone interviews. It was nearly 7 P.M. before she was able to switch off her screen, relax, and grab a bite to eat. She left the newsroom and wearily trudged down the hallway to the elevator, taking the jolting ride to the cafeteria.

Her stomach growled "Get me food!" all the way up to the tenth floor. She strode into the cafeteria, bypassed the salad bar, and zeroed in on the grill. The gangly Mexican cook, dwarfed by a white hat resembling a mushroom cloud, greeted her with a cheerful grin.

Mordente placed her order hurriedly in Spanish, asking him for two grilled turkey and cheese sandwiches. While he prepared her sandwiches, she whirled around the circular buffet, snatching a handful of chocolate chip cookies, a bag of Doritos, and a tall Styrofoam soft drink cup full of black coffee.

She took her sandwiches with a thankful smile, rushed through the cashier's line, and settled down to eat at a table by a window. The moment her rear end touched the seat and her nose took in the aroma of the hot food, she could feel herself beginning to unwind. Outside, she could see the red numbers on the *Times* building clock glowing against the dark backdrop of the Civic Center buildings. Today, she realized, had felt like a week.

Her stomach took control of her body now, ordering her to grab a sandwich and wolf it down in six hungry bites. She did. Mordente had learned long ago how to handle her body. She knew she could occasionally put her stomach on hold for an entire day, but when the food was on the table, she had to let her stomach call the shots. That was the deal she had struck with her stomach. She understood her body and had worked out agreements with her bowels, hair, bladder, teeth, uterus and, most importantly, her lower back.

The quick consumption of sandwich number one had taken the edge off her hunger and her stomach allowed her to approach the rest of the meal in a more relaxed manner. Sipping her coffee, which was so hot it nearly scalded her tongue, she folded open the paper to the Metro section.

She scanned the narrow story running down the first column about the robbery of another bank by a gang who hid their faces with rubber Halloween masks. This bank was robbed, it seemed, by Yoda, Jimmy Carter, and a werewolf. She glanced at a feature photo of an elderly woman in a wheelchair rolling down the street, a duck on a leash following along.

Mid-page, just under the fold, she found her lengthy round-up of southland wind damage. She read it with a sense of mild achievement and a renewed feeling of fatigue.

She was about ready to follow the story to the jump when she saw the tiny, boxed article below hers. It was just a glorified filler, so unimportant that no by-line was attributed to it, but she looked at it anyway. Sometimes these short stories were interesting.

VENICE—A Hollywood nurse was killed Wednesday morning by an exploding bomb rigged to the ignition system of her boyfriend's car.

Cheshire Davis, 32, was leaving the home of 35-year-old Brett Macklin at about 6 A.M. when the blast occurred. Police say she triggered the bomb when she tried to start his car, a vintage 1959 Cadillac.

The blaze resulting from the explosion was quickly contained by firefighters before it could do more than superficial damage to Macklin's home.

A police spokesman said there is no apparent motive for the bombing and, refusing to venture an explanation of any kind, noted an investigation is under way. Macklin is owner and operator of Blue Yonder Airways in Santa Monica and has no history, according to police sources, of any "criminal associations."

The early morning blast jolted residents living as far as two miles away from Macklin's home, police say.

Mordente felt that annoying tingle between her shoulder blades that told her there was something more to the story than she caught at first glance.

She read the story again. *So, maybe one of 'em had a jilted lover that tried to get even.* The tingle didn't fade. Mordente gave the story a third going over, wondering what it was about the article that nagged at her.

Then it hit her. That name … *Macklin* … she had heard it somewhere before. She got up, her hunger forgotten, and dashed down the stairwell to the *Times* morgue.

The smoke from the fire was trapped in Brett Macklin's house. It clung to the walls, his body, the furniture. Everything he ate or drank in the house tasted charred.

He spent the morning moving aimlessly through the house, trying to hide from it. But the smell was everywhere. And so was Cheshire. Everywhere he turned he was confronted by her presence—the houseplants Cheshire had brought over and nurtured; the dishtowels she had made while they watched old movies on TV together; her makeup scattered on the bathroom counter top; her comforter, covered with broken glass, in a heap on the bed.

Macklin felt smothered, on the verge of screaming. Death was everywhere, closing in on him. Yet he couldn't leave the house. Something kept him there. He picked up the glass, shard by shard, from the bedroom and made the bed. He got down on his hands and knees and scrubbed the chocolate ice cream off the kitchen floor. He cleaned the house like a robot, unthinking, performing the tasks as if controlled by some irreversible computer program.

By late afternoon, there was nothing else to clean, nowhere to hide. He was forced to feel. He felt the coldness gradually sweep over him, numbing the dull ache of sadness as it had months before.

He paced in the living room. The coldness inside him was melting under the searing heat of a new emotion. It scorched through him, fed by his sadness. It flushed his skin, tightened his face muscles, and quickened his heartbeat.

His depression was gone, beaten. A familiar voice spoke to him again.

Make them pay.

Macklin rebounded, snapping out of his depressed lethargy. He called up a local rent-a-car place and had them deliver a full-size Chevrolet Impala. He took the Glad bag filled with Saputo's trash, put it in the trunk, and drove to K-Mart, where he bought a pair of plastic gloves to examine the typewriter ribbons.

While mother nature drop-kicked transients into the Pacific Ocean, crushed European luxury cars, and swatted homes off the Hollywood hills, Macklin was sitting alone in the cavernous Blue Yonder hangar at the Santa Monica Airport, wading through Saputo's trash.

First, he studied everything that had been typed on the ribbons by reading them backward, following the three lines of letters in a W-shaped trail and jotting them down on a legal pad.

The ribbon contained memos to kiddie porn distributors that promised new films within several weeks and a regular production schedule. Also, Macklin read through sales copy for the kiddie porn films and products:

"... *Kiddie Call Girls, Moppet Cock Suckers,* and *Cuddly Clit* offer the demanding man *hot* child sexuality at its erotic best..."

"... lifelike Latex blow up dolls with warm vaginas and budding tits that make them the best lay imaginable ... whenever you want it!"

"... they're young, they're wet, they're 200 glossy black and white pictures of the horniest sweet candy *ever*..."

Macklin stared down at the legal pad, then glanced at the remaining stacks of papers, photos, and film. Bile, hot and acidic, bubbled up in his throat. He dashed to the bathroom, leaned over the toilet, and vomited in deep, aching heaves that left him light-headed and shaky-kneed.

Bracing himself against the sink, he straightened up and flushed the toilet. He felt as if he had puked up everything except his heart and lungs. He turned on the faucet, cupped his hands under the cool water, and splashed his face a few times. Then, his face damp, he meekly ventured a look at himself in the mirror.

His skin was chalk-white, the only tinge of color came from the dark circles that underscored his eyes and gave them a sunken, empty look. Macklin splashed his face again, as if he could wash the face he saw in the mirror off his own.

Dabbing his face dry with a rough paper towel, Macklin shuffled back into the hangar and decided to forget the piles of paper for a while and see what the film strips had to offer. Best to do it on an empty stomach, he thought. All I can do is gag.

He sat down on a stool and fed the torn strips of celluloid, which he presumed were outtakes, rejects, and damaged film, through his tiny Super 8 viewer. The same viewer he had used to edit home movies he shot of Cory. Brooke nursing Cory at the hospital. Cory walking for the first time. His father playing with Cory, she nearly hidden under J. D. Macklin's LAPD hat. Cory's seventh birthday party at Disneyland.

He spent the next two hours in front of the editor. Most of the film was outtake footage for a good reason. The endless yards of blurry, indiscernible shots and scratched film had made Macklin's eyes stinging red. Macklin yawned, tired of the vague shapes, overexposed film, and lingering shots of genitalia.

Macklin wearily fed another three-foot-long strip of film quickly through the editor. Something bright flashed for a split second on the tiny screen, catching his attention. He pulled the strip backward, careful not to rip the sprockets on the feed. Another bright flash amidst the blur of frames. Macklin brought the film through again slowly and stopped at the bright frame.

The shot was hazy, but in comparison to the rest of the film, it was Oscar-winning cinematography. A young girl, perhaps ten years old, sat on a stool, her legs crossed, at the edge of a movie set. It must be a wild shot, Macklin thought, taken accidentally and not part of their movie. Lights and rafters, as well as several people, could be made out in the background.

She looked serene, calm.

Not like she would be, Macklin thought. Not swollen and green, naked and covered in mud. Not rotting beside a rain-swelled canal.

Macklin clicked off the editor. *Not dead.*

A loud rapping at the hangar door startled him. Macklin, tearing the frame from the strip and putting it in his shirt pocket, quickly swept everything on the table into the Glad bag.

The knocking became irritated and persistent.

"Hang on!" Macklin yelled as he dragged the bag along the floor into his darkened office. He closed the office door and sprinted across the hangar. Macklin took a deep breath and opened the door.

A gust of cold wind blew into the hangar. Standing against the night, under a narrow cone of light cast by a dirty bulb above the door, was a dark-skinned woman in khaki pants, a white woven silk blazer, and brown blouse.

She looked at him with curious green eyes that sparkled like olivine stones. "Brett Macklin?"

"Yes?"

"My name is Jessica Mordente," she said politely. "I'm with the *Los Angeles Times.*"

A fucking reporter, Macklin thought, a vulture.

"I've got a subscription," Macklin said curtly, closing the door. She jammed her foot in the way, forcing the door open a crack.

"Good. Then you'll see the story that exposes Mr. Jury."

Macklin's stomach muscles tightened defensively as if he were preparing to ward off a blow. "Move your foot, lady, or you're going to lose it." Macklin stared into her eyes and felt a tremor of nervousness at the determination he saw there. A sense of apprehension squeezed him, viselike. He'd be damned, though, if he'd give up any ground. "I'm in no mood for journalistic bullshit."

"Come now, Mr. Macklin, couldn't we talk for just a moment?" she said with exaggerated care, as if talking to a temperamental child. It made Macklin want to throttle her. "Aren't you even a little interested in Mr. Jury?"

"Not the slightest."

Mordente shook her head and spoke evenly. "I think you are, Mr. Macklin. Very much." She met his scornful gaze. "Mr. Jury's first victims were the men suspected of killing your father. Interesting, huh?"

"He made a good choice."

"Now someone has planted a bomb in your car and killed your girlfriend." She saw Macklin's face harden. "I think Mr. Jury is going to strike again, real soon."

"And I think you're about to acquire a permanent limp."

Mordente laughed coyly. "Well, Mr. Macklin, a polite good night to you, too." She turned her back to him and walked away, waving her hand at him. "See you around."

Macklin slammed the door shut and fell back against it. His heart raced. The world was closing in on him again. Harder this time. Macklin took several deep breaths, exhaling them slowly, trying to calm himself. *I don't care if they find out who I am, what I am.*

Then why are you so rattled, Macky boy?

Macklin pulled the piece of film out of his pocket and studied it.

Because I don't want anyone to stop me until I've evened the score.

CHAPTER SEVEN

Erica Tandy stretched her legs out as far as they could go and tried to touch the darkish cloud with her toes. She almost made it, but the swing resisted at the height of its climb. The swing fell back and she tucked her legs, trying to grab the air and pin it between her calves and the underside of her thighs.

It was Friday, the second clear day after so many rainy days when she couldn't come out and play. She had the whole muddy park to herself. It was chilly, but the crisp wind cooled the perspiration, prompted by her energetic swinging, that she could feel on her back.

As she swung backward over the ground, she looked down at the big hole in the dirt, carved out by the dozens of kids who dragged their feet as they rode the swing. It was brimming over with dirty water, so she bent her legs closer to her to prevent her toes from skimming the puddle.

The swing carried Erica back, high up into the air again. The swing froze for a split second and then fell forward. She extended her legs, tightened her grip on the chain, and felt the swing race downward and begin its climb toward the sky.

It stopped with a jolt that flung her face forward toward the dirt. She grasped the chains tightly, holding herself in the swing. Angrily, she whipped her head around to see what had so suddenly halted her skyward arc.

Erica saw a man standing behind her, holding the chain above her hands. At first she was scared because he looked like that awful man called Mr. Dark she had seen in that spooky movie on HBO. She remembered Mr. Dark had these pictures of kids on his palms and would squeeze his hands real hard until blood dripped out of his fists. "Hi there," the man said, smiling warmly. He brought the swing down to him slowly. She kept her eyes on his. She didn't like his thin eyes at all. They were too far into his head as if they were trying to hide from her or something. "Your mom told me I'd find you here."

"Why?" she asked, stepping shakily off the swing. The man glided around in front of her. She became powerfully aware of the enormity of the park and the absence of any other children. It made her chilly, even though the red sweater Nana had made her for Christmas should have kept her warm.

"Because she has a special lunch planned." He put his hand on her shoulder. His black-gloved hand felt heavy, like an iron clasp. "A party."

"A party?" she asked shyly. She felt him guide her away from the swing set toward the street.

"With cookies and cake." He walked up beside her, his hand firmly grasping her shoulder. "A surprise party for ..." He let his voice trail off.

"For Daddy?" She eagerly filled the conversational lapse.

"Yes," he agreed in a praising tone. "For your father."

The fear, like a cloud that had obscured the sun, floated away and she felt warm again. Surprising Dad would be fun! The stranger's eyes didn't look so bad now. Instead of Mr. Dark, he was beginning to look like Rick Springfield, though she had never seen Rick dressed like this, with a big scarf and overcoat.

"You have a van just like my uncle's," she said. He reached past her and opened the van's passenger door.

"He helped me pick it out." Tice smiled. She climbed in, and he closed the door behind her.

Shaw stood very still in the center of Macklin's living room, holding a magnifying glass over his eye with one hand and a strip of movie film up to the light with the other.

"It's Orlock," Shaw whispered.

Macklin barely heard him. "What did you say?"

"In the background, behind the girl." Shaw lowered his arms and faced Macklin. "Crocker Orlock is standing there."

"Great." Macklin clapped Shaw on the back. "Nail the son of a bitch, then give me a few seconds alone with him and I'll find out who killed Cheshire."

"Hold on, Mack." Shaw held the film out to Macklin. "We can't get him yet."

"Why the hell not?" Macklin shouted into Shaw's face. "What more do you need? It's all there on the film. For God's sake, Ronny, you've got Orlock with a kidnapped girl who turned up dead."

Shaw tossed the magnifying glass on the couch and ran his hand through his hair. "Mack, this film is virtually useless. It doesn't prove a thing."

"Ronny, are you out of your mind? What's the matter with you?" Macklin yanked the film from Shaw's hand and waved it in front of the detective's face. "Look at this closely. It links Orlock with everything. Murder. Kiddie porn. Do I have to gift-wrap him and drop him off at police headquarters for you?"

Shaw jabbed the film with his index finger. "You're gonna have to do better than that. It won't stand up in court. For starters, it's illegally obtained evidence—"

"So say it was given to you by an anonymous good samaritan," Macklin interrupted impatiently, a scowl of frustration on his face.

"Number two," Shaw continued, ignoring Macklin's remark, "we can't positively identify Orlock. The more we blow it up, the blurrier it will get. His attorney can talk a jury out of this with ease."

"You know it's Orlock! You recognized him!" Macklin yelled.

"Yeah, so what! Grow up, Mack. Truth can be disproved by a good lawyer living off a fat retainer," Shaw sighed. "Thirdly, even if we can convince the jury it's Orlock, we can't prove he kidnapped her. Look, what the film does prove is that Crocker is dirty."

"You knew that already, Ronny."

"But now I *know* that."

Macklin fell back wearily against the wall and slid down into a sitting position on the floor facing Shaw, who stood in front of the fireplace. "Okay, did you get anything from the list of plates I gave you?"

"Yeah, that paid off. The warehouse is owned by Orlock through a maze of dummy companies and leased to Saputo by an independent, legitimate rental agency. The van also belongs to Orlock, as does the Seville you saw Saputo driving."

Macklin looked up at Shaw and spoke very carefully. "I think it's time Mr. Jury takes care of it."

"Really?" Shaw smirked. "Remember your grandiose speech about due process?"

Macklin nodded.

"Does it still hold, or do you run out of here now, guns blazing?"

Macklin stared silently at Shaw for a full minute. "It still holds."

"Good." Shaw pulled a slip of paper out of his pocket and tossed it into Macklin's lap. "He's expecting you."

Shaw went to the front door and walked out.

Macklin glanced at the crumpled paper in his lap and picked it up. He unfolded it slowly and read it twice.

Harlan Fitz. 555-9182

Whenever life got complicated, Harlan Fitz sought refuge in the Greasy Spoon, where club sandwiches start at $6.50 and chocolate ice cream is white.

The bookcase-lined walls made him feel like he was back in his judge's chambers, and the aroma of cooking food gave the popular Century City restaurant a warm, homey quality that he found relaxing.

The Greasy Spoon was nestled between what Fitz would have called two 20-story stereo speakers; the dressed-for-success executives knew them as the Twin Towers, two silver monoliths rising above the exclusive cluster of office buildings just outside Beverly Hills.

Fitz sat at his favorite table, tucked into a shadowy corner in the back and nursed a Bloody Mary while watching the ebb and flow of the Friday noontime crowd. He could hear the rumble of the Santa Ana's sweeping through the city, which had been lulled into complacency by a deceptively calm morning.

The usually trim, slim, and prim Century City executives emerged at noon like preprogrammed robots from their high-rent, high-rise offices and marched into the Greasy Spoon looking mop-topped and harried. Fitz noticed that even actor Peter Graves, huddled amongst the crowd awaiting tables, appeared disheveled. Having seen *Mission Impossible,* Fitz knew how rare *that* was.

Fitz ordered a second drink and glanced nervously at his watch. He was watching for the mysterious vigilante to show up and half hoping the man wouldn't. He didn't kid himself. Just agreeing to meet with Mr. Jury and not going to the police made him an accomplice. But then again, if Shaw was any indication, the LAPD wouldn't give a damn anyway.

He buttered a pencil-thin breadstick and noticed, uneasily, that his hand was shaking just a bit. Fitz couldn't decide whether what he felt was fear or excitement.

Macklin sat at the bar, as he had for the last two hours, watching Fitz across the room and glancing at faces, hunting for anyone who might be a cop or reporter waiting to snare Mr. Jury in a nice trap.

When Macklin spotted Peter Graves, he almost bolted out of the restaurant. For a split second fiction became reality for him and he thought the *Mission Impossible* team had come to get him.

Shit, Macky boy, take it easy. Macklin swallowed the remainder of his beer, slid off his barstool, and headed toward Fitz's table, a manila envelope under his arm.

Macklin neared the round table. "Excuse me, are you Judge Fitz?"

Fitz's head shot up quickly, the voice startling him. He studied the approaching man and found himself squinting back at the blue eyes that were unabashedly sizing him up.

"Yes," Fitz replied, recovering his composure, and motioned to the seat in front of him. "You must be—" Fitz cut himself off and shrugged "—the mystery man."

Macklin's stony expression was broken by an ironic grin. He folded his six-foot frame into the padded wicker chair and offered Fitz his hand as he sat down. "My name's Brett Macklin."

Fitz straightened up in his seat and shook Macklin's hand. Macklin's grip was strong and firm, giving Fitz the impression that Macklin was a man who was self-assured and aggressive, a fighter. Or, Fitz wondered, am I just reaffirming my preconceived notions?

"You must be as nervous as I am, Mr. Macklin."

Macklin nodded, setting the envelope in his lap. "More."

"Have any trouble finding me?"

"Not at all. You said look for the darkest corner of the restaurant and you'd be in it." Macklin shrugged. "You were right. Besides, I caught a few minutes of your show on TV before I came."

A freckled, pale-skinned waitress, her ample girth bound by a nannyish black apron, came to the table. "I see your friend has arrived, Judge. Are you ready to order?"

"I'll have another Bloody Mary, thanks," Fitz replied.

"Scotch on the rocks," Macklin said. The waitress nodded at them both and bustled toward the bar.

Fitz leaned back in his seat, watching the waitress go, and chuckled. "Why did I expect you to ask for the drink in a dirty glass?"

Macklin shifted uneasily in his seat. "I didn't come here to trade one-liners with you. This isn't easy for me."

Fitz was about to speak when the waitress appeared again, giving them their drinks. The judge took a sip of his drink and then stirred it with his swizzle stick.

"Mr. Macklin, are you at all familiar with California history?"

"Slightly," Macklin said wearily, lifting his glass to his lips.

"In the mid-eighteen hundreds, San Francisco was being eaten alive by crime. The police, the courts, the city government, they were all thoroughly infected by corruption and did nothing. The citizenry took to the streets themselves, hunting down criminals, conducting trials, and then strictly punishing the offenders." Fitz took another sip of his drink and regarded Macklin solemnly. "Popular opinion then, and now, is quite supportive of those vigilantes. An opinion leader of the era, a seaman-turned-lawyer named Richard Henry Dana, said the vigilantes rescued the city, restoring morality and good government."

Fitz smiled, meeting Macklin's gaze. "He said the vigilantes were," his voice took on a high, melodramatic tone as he quoted from memory " 'the last resort of the thinking and the good, taken to only when vice, fraud and ruffianism have intrenched themselves behind the forms of law, suffrage and ballot, and there is no hope but in organized force whose action must be instant and thorough.' "

Macklin saw the judge's hand tighten into a fist on the table. "Mr. Macklin, I believe that same environment, that same laxity of the law, exists today. It sickens me. And until now I've felt helpless to stop it. Your desire for due process proves what I suspected before, that you aren't a murderer, but a man of principle trying to restore order."

Macklin looked around the room, afraid someone might have overheard. None of the patrons seemed to be paying any attention to them. "Can we take a walk? I really don't feel comfortable talking here."

Fitz laughed self-consciously. "Of course. Forgive me. I wanted to at least meet here, on familiar ground, where I could feel comfortable. This was the only place I could think of besides home, and that's always out. I never bring work home. That is my sanctuary. I will not let it be touched by matters like this."

Macklin nodded somberly. His home could never be a sanctuary, not now. Every facet of his life had been irrevocably touched by the disease that took his father first, then Cheshire. Slowly but surely, he knew, it was infecting him as well.

They left the restaurant and were struck by a strong gust of wind that whipped up their hair as they made their way to the escalator. They didn't talk as they rode it down to the second floor of the parking garage.

Macklin breathed through his mouth. The garage was thick with car exhaust fumes trapped inside the structure by the raging winds. Their footsteps echoed through the dark garage as they walked silently between aisles of parked cars to Fitz's metallic blue two-door '79 Buick Regal. Fitz unlocked the passenger door, motioned Macklin inside, and then walked around and got in as well.

"There, now we have some privacy." Fitz put his key in the ignition, twisted it to the alternator setting, and then turned on the stereo. Classical music played softly over the speakers. "First,

I need to know a little more about you. How did you become a vigilante?"

Macklin told his story, beginning with his father's death and ending with his surveillance of Wesley Saputo, glossing over Cheshire's murder without knowing why. He kept the encounter with Mordente to himself, as he had with Shaw. He thought it was pointless to scare either of them.

"I see," Fitz said quietly. "What kind of material evidence have you collected?"

Macklin handed Fitz the envelope. "These memos and a strip of film that shows Orlock with a child the police later found raped and strangled."

Fitz lifted the flap and thumbed through the items in the envelope, his face hardening.

When the judge got to the film strip and held it up to the interior light, Macklin spoke up. "Shaw tells me he can make out Crocker Orlock in the background. He says that isn't enough to prove Orlock's complicity."

Fitz grunted. "He's right, I'm afraid. I need more evidence that ties Orlock directly to the films and thereby the murders." He returned the envelope to Macklin. "The problem is all the evidence against Orlock will be circumstantial. To make up for that, I need a preponderance of evidence to feel comfortable finding guilt."

"You want more evidence." Macklin opened the car door. "I'll get it. What about Saputo?"

"He should never have been released from jail," Fitz responded, staring out the windshield at the rows of parked cars. "Your evidence, coupled with what Sergeant Shaw told me, leaves no doubt in my mind that Saputo is back in business. In time, it might be possible to gather evidence that can be used in a courtroom, but even then I don't know if a conviction could be secured or if he'd even remain behind bars."

Fitz started the engine and then glanced at Macklin. "So shut the bastard down."

CHAPTER EIGHT

Richard Nixon and Darth Vader held Uzis and stood in the bed of the pickup truck E.T. had just driven through the bank's plate-glass window.

"Everyone face down on the floor," Nixon yelled over the shrill alarm. "If I see anyone's face, I'll blow it off."

The nine lunch-hour customers and the dozen bank employees didn't argue with the three men in the rubber masks. Everyone in the convex, window-walled bank lobby dropped to their knees and flattened themselves on the glass-strewn floor.

E.T. left the truck's engine running and bolted from the cab. He vaulted over the bank counter and moved quickly to each teller's window, stuffing handfuls of money into a large gunney sack.

Darth Vader, standing in the truck's bed with Nixon, caught a movement on the floor. An old lady was raising her head. "Get down!" he barked.

"I can't," she whined, looking up. "There's a sharp piece of glass tha—"

Vader squeezed the trigger of his Uzi. Her body stuttered back along the floor; bullets bit into her head and spit out blood. Fearful screams from the panicked employees and customers joined the frenzied wail of the alarm.

"Goddamnit, why did you do that?" Nixon shouted. "C'mon, we've got enough cash, let's get out of here!"

"I don't believe I saw you boys sign a withdrawal slip." A voice behind the three robbers stopped them cold. They turned and saw Brett Macklin standing in the doorway, the .357 Magnum at his side.

Macklin caught a jerk in E.T.'s gun arm, crouched and spun on his heels, firing twice. The slugs punched into E.T.'s stomach, lifting him up and tossing him back into a row of desks.

Macklin then threw himself sideways as Nixon raked the doorway with retaliatory gunfire. The bullets chased Macklin, shattering the glass above his head as he scrambled behind the bank counter. The customers quivered on the floor, the staccato beat of gunfire echoing in their ears.

Vader climbed into the driver's seat of the truck, shifted it into drive, and pressed the accelerator to the floor. The truck shot forward, knocking Nixon off balance. Macklin popped up behind the counter and fired.

The bullets slapped Nixon off the moving truck and sent him toppling backward into a potted palm. Macklin strode from behind the counter just as the truck smashed through the plate-glass window on the opposite end of the bank. Raising his gun arm, Macklin looked down the length of his barrel at the truck screeching madly south on Century Park East. And then he squeezed the trigger.

The truck burst apart in a red-orange thunderclap of flame, gnarled metal and glass shards streaking through the air. Macklin shoved the gun under his waistband, pulled his leather jacket over it, and rushed out of the bank just as it erupted into chaos, the frightened people on the floor clambering to their feet.

He dashed onto the sidewalk and trotted up the street against the current of Century City businessmen charging to the bank. His heart was racing and his body was drenched in sweat.

It had all happened so fast. He was driving out of the parking garage across the street when he spotted the robbery taking place. He screeched to a stop a few yards from the bank, grabbed his Magnum, and ran inside.

His only regret now was that he arrived too late to save the elderly woman. Macklin got into his car, which he had left double-parked and still running, and sped away from the bank, glancing in his rear-view mirror at the blazing truck and the growing crowd of people in his wake.

Macklin steered the Impala into the left-turn lane onto the westbound stretch of Santa Monica Boulevard. At the same moment three police cars, sirens blaring, skidded behind him onto Century Park East and raced to the bank. Breathing deeply with relief, Macklin pulled the gun out of his waistband, tossed it into the glovebox, and slammed it shut.

Jessica Mordente swung her legs over the yellow tape, marked DO NOT ENTER, that surrounded the bank and stepped carefully through the shattered window.

Broken glass crunched under her heels as she strolled across the lobby, listening to the rumble of voices that filled the bank. Flashbulbs on LAPD cameras spit light into various corners of the glass-walled lobby. Uniformed officers and detectives were scattered about in huddles, interviewing the bank employees and customers. To Mordente's left, beyond the teller's counter, she saw men in white lift a black body bag onto a stretcher.

She carefully stepped around the blood-specked chalk outline of a body drawn on the floor and headed toward a familiar face. FBI Special Agent Chet Navarro stood at the other end of the room, half-turned toward the street, where firefighters hosed down the streaming, blackened remains of the pickup truck.

Mordente admired Navarro's lean physique, well displayed in a tailored gray suit. Her eyes lingered on his firm, strong legs and followed them up to his tight, round buttocks, nicely hugged by pleated slacks. She remembered how soft that fine ass felt squeezed in her hands.

She pressed her hand against the small of his back. "How's my favorite Fed?"

Navarro turned, surprised. "Jessie, how did you get in here?"

She smiled. "Does it matter?" Glancing past him, she could see the bank camera mounted high on a pillar.

"No," he said, slipping his arm around her shoulder and steering her outside. "I haven't seen you for quite a while."

"Can you believe this place?" she asked. They walked through the broken window onto the sidewalk. "It looks like a small war took place here."

"A small war *did*," Navarro replied, unbuttoning his collar and loosening his tie with his free hand. They followed the black skid marks left by the truck to the street. "Some good samaritan blew the fuck out of the rubber-mask gang. So now you can take your life savings out of your mattress and put it in the bank again."

"Anyone see this good samaritan?" she asked.

"No, everyone was lying face down on the floor."

She stopped and stared into his amber eyes. "What about the bank camera?"

"What about it? You know, I've missed you, Jessie." He put his hands in his pockets and looked around self-consciously. "You're impossible to reach."

She stepped closer so that he could feel her breath on him. "I've missed you too, Chet. Maybe we could get together. Tell me, do you think you got a picture of the mystery man?"

"I don't know."

"I'd like to see it," she said softly.

"Jessie." He started walking toward the street again, stopping at the barrier of yellow tape. "You know I can't let you print the photo unless the Bureau clears it first."

She caught up with him. "Who said anything about printing it? I just want to *see* it."

Navarro frowned, swung his legs over the yellow tape, and held out his hand to help Mordente over. "I don't think so. I could get in a lot of trouble, Jessie."

She took his hand and climbed over the tape. "I don't want you to get in any trouble," she said, squeezing his hand reassuringly. "But I would like to see the photo. And I'd like to see you, too. It's been a long time, hasn't it, Chet?"

"How about dinner?" he asked tentatively.

"Sure, we can have dinner at my place." She patted him gently on the side and walked away. "I'll give you a call to see how your investigation is going."

As she walked to her Mazda RX7, she felt Navarro's eyes on her. It made her feel attractive. And powerful. She knew she'd get that photo somehow, and she had a strong hunch about the face she'd see staring back at her from it.

"Orlock residence, who's calling, please?" The voice sounded to Brett Macklin like an eerie cross between Jack Palance and Charles Bronson.

"John Smith," Macklin replied sarcastically. "Give me Orlock."

"I'm sorry, he's busy right now," the man said politely, then, more sternly, "I'll take a message."

It was a command, not a considerate offer.

"Take this down, buddy. Tell Orlock to get on the phone or his kid porn operation will be on the front page of tomorrow's *Times*."

"It's all right, Tice," another voice intruded on the line. "I'll deal with the gentleman." Macklin heard a click as Tice hung up his extension. "All right, Mr., ah, Smith, what can I do for you?"

"Listen, that's what. You and I are about to become partners in the candy business."

"I'm not in the candy business, Mr. Smith."

"Don't screw around with me, Orlock. I'd just as soon step on you than deal with you, but the eastern interests I represent don't share my opinion of you."

Orlock laughed. "C'mon, Mr. Smith, this is ridiculous. I'm a very busy man, with no time for poor James Cagney impersonations. Just who are you and what are you talking about?"

"Let's meet and discuss that."

Orlock sighed. "Good-bye, Mr. Smi—"

"I'm looking at this photograph of you," Macklin interrupted. "It's quite amusing. Maybe you know the one. You're standing behind a little girl."

Macklin paused to let his words sink in. "A little girl who a short time later was found face down in a canal, bloated, her neck broken. I'm sure the district attorney and the *Times* would love copies of the picture. What do you think, Orlock?"

"Perhaps I can juggle a few appointments and chat with you," Orlock said. "Where and when would you like to get together?"

"Your warehouse in Culver City. I want to see your operation."

"I have no operation, as you call it, Mr. Smith. I rent the warehouse to various—"

"Seven o'clock tonight." Macklin slammed the phone down. The clap echoed through the empty hangar. He plucked the black suction mike, purchased for just a buck or two at Radio Shack, from the telephone receiver and clicked off the cassette recorder it was attached to. There was nothing incriminating on the tape, but it was nice to have.

Macklin leaned back in his torn vinyl office chair, rested his feet on his paper-cluttered desk, and gazed through the doorway at his Jet Ranger helicopter and his Cessna in the hangar. I'm a pilot not a cop, he told himself. What the hell am I doing?

But he knew that as exciting and beautiful and relaxing as flying was for him, there was something essential missing that prevented him from feeling content with his life, something he once had when he was on the UCLA track team. It was a sense of utterly consuming physical challenge, of pushing his limitations to the point of agony. The pain always ebbed, though, and left an afterglow of exhilaration that charged him until the next challenge, when he would give just a little bit more.

In the Quick Stop market. In the bank today. He had felt that charge, that sweet addictive charge, again. *Admit it, Macky boy. It's never felt better...*

Macklin swung his feet off the table, knocking stacks of paper to the floor.

"Shit." He bent over and spent a moment attempting to assemble the papers before giving up and kicking them. Paper scattered around the room, settling on the floor and chairs and boxes and cabinets like giant, mutated snowflakes.

He punched the door and walked into the hangar.

It's no life, no matter how good it might feel, Macklin lectured to himself. A man can't live that way.

We'll see .... a voice inside chided him.

"Hey, Brett, what the hell happened to your house?"

Macklin turned and at first glance didn't recognize the man coming in the hangar wearing reflecting sunglasses, pink satin scalloped shirt, and designer jeans.

"Mort?" Macklin asked incredulously.

"Of course it's me." As Mort came closer, Macklin noticed his friend's uncharacteristically dark tan and the cloud of Pierre Cardin aftershave that surrounded him. "But not for long. I'm nearly Mortimer Neville."

"You're nearly out of your mind. What is all this shit?"

Mort patted himself on the rear. "One pair of Sassoon jeans." He tapped the rim of his glasses. "Porsche shades." He ran his hand down the scallop cut of his shirt. "One genuine Morey Geyer scalloped shirt from Palm Springs, and, to top it all off," Mort unbuttoned his collar to expose his hairless chest "a summer tan from Al Bonzer's Sunset Strip tanning boutique."

Macklin groaned. "Jesus, Mort, you look ridiculous."

"Listen, Brett, your opinion doesn't count. You have no taste." Mort took off his sunglasses, folded them, and slipped them into his breast pocket. "Cheshire does. I went by the place to model my threads for her first and get a *real* opinion, but I couldn't find her. What happened to the place anyway? It's scorched."

Macklin suddenly realized Mort *didn't know,* that his friend had only been back in Los Angeles for a few hours.

"Hey, Brett, what's wrong?" Mort said, the glow disappearing from his face. "You look like you're about to puke."

Macklin didn't know how to begin. There was no right way. "Mort, she's dead."

"Huh?"

"Cheshire, she's been murdered." Macklin grasped Mort's shoulder. "Someone put a bomb in my car and she was blown up."

Mort squinted his eyes quizzically and tilted his head toward Macklin. "What?"

"Cheshire is dead," Macklin said carefully.

Mort swatted Macklin's arm away. "It's you, isn't it?"

"What?" Macklin snapped.

"Mr. Jury. The killing. It isn't over, is it?" Mort glared at Macklin. "IS IT!?" he yelled.

Macklin frowned and exhaled slowly. "No it isn't, Mort. I'm not sure it ever will be."

Without warning, Mort smashed his fist into Macklin's stomach and, before Macklin could recover, followed through with an uppercut that sent Macklin sprawling onto the floor.

"Fuck you, Brett, just fuck you."

Turning his back to Macklin, Mort walked toward the hangar door.

"Mort," Macklin rasped, propping himself up on his elbows. "Wait, I need your help!"

Mort kept walking.

"Damnit, Mort, I loved her too!"

Mort stopped, his shoulders sagging.

Macklin stood up shakily. "We can make them pay, Mort. Together."

Mort looked over his shoulder. "Who are *they*?"

"A bunch of psychos who kidnap kids, force them to have sex in porno movies, and then kill them." Macklin held out his hand to him. "Will you help me?"

Mort turned around slowly and sighed. Macklin waited, his hand out.

"Please?" Macklin prodded.

Mort nodded, reached out, and shook Macklin's hand. "I'm sorry I hit you. I was pissed. I know it isn't your fault."

"It's all right, I don't blame you. I thought it was over too."

Macklin told Mort about his meeting with Stocker and Shaw, the surveillance of Saputo, his meeting earlier that day with Harlan Fitz, and the phone call he had just made to Orlock.

"What do you want me to do?" Mort asked.

"I want you on the roof of the building across from the warehouse, taking pictures and covering me," Macklin said. "If I get into trouble, call Shaw."

"All right."

"You have a gun, don't you?"

Mort hedged with silence. He hadn't used a gun since his alcoholic days on the LAPD chopper patrol.

"Yes or no, Mort? Do you have a gun?" Macklin knew Mort had been a crack shot once and thought he probably wasn't too bad now.

"Yes," Mort said. "But, Mack, I haven't fired a gun since—"

"No arguments," Macklin interrupted. "It will protect both of us."

Macklin yanked a pen out of his breast pocket. "Gimme a piece of paper, Mort."

Mort pulled a wrinkled Blue Yonder Airways business card out of his back pocket and handed it to him. Macklin glanced at the card, gave Mort a disapproving look, and turned it over.

"Here's where I'm meeting Orlock." He scribbled down directions and gave the card back to Mort.

"It's a date," Mort said, studying the card.

"Good, then I'll see you tonight." Macklin headed toward the door.

"Wait a minute, Brett."

Macklin turned around.

"If they put a bomb in your car, they must know who you are," Mort said. "They must know you're not a representative of some eastern syndicate."

"I don't think they ever saw my face," Macklin replied. "My hunch is they saw me tailing Saputo, got my license number, and didn't bother to do any other checking before they decided to play it safe and kill me."

"And what if you're wrong?" Mort argued. "What if they know you're just a cocky pilot?"

"I'll have to stay alive long enough for you to rescue me."

CHAPTER NINE

Shaw sat on the edge of his couch and leaned close to the portable black and white TV, which was sitting on a blue plastic milk crate in the center of the living room.

Tuxedo-clad superspy Pete Cypher stood in the underground garage of his apartment building watching three sword-swinging Ninja warriors kick his blazing red Corvette convertible into a pile of fiberglass dust.

"As you can see, Mr. Cypher, we mean business." The portly Frenchman in the wheelchair grinned, stroking the chameleon in his lap. "Where is the electrofremeon nodule?"

Cypher arched his eyebrows in mock surprise. "I thought you knew." He shot a glance at the rubble that had once been his car. "It was in the glove compartment."

"Oh, Pete Cypher is smooth," Shaw whispered, glancing over his shoulder at his white girlfriend. "C'mon, Sunshine, you gotta see this. Cypher is gonna flatten these guys any second now with his laser ring or his flame-throwing shoe."

"Uh-huh," she mumbled without looking up from her paperback copy of *Loose Change*. Curled up in a red vinyl bean bag, Sunshine was braless in her gauze blouse, her long brown hair falling across her chest and clear down to her Indian wraparound skirt.

Shaw shrugged, decided it was her loss, and stared intently at the screen again.

"Very amusing, Mr. Cypher," the Frenchman quipped, "but that isn't reason enough to keep you alive. I want it now."

Cypher grinned. "Then I'll just have to give it to you."

Shaw laughed. "Here it comes, Sunny. Cypher is gonna do his thing."

"Uh-huh," Sunshine replied.

Someone knocked at Shaw's door.

"Shit. Sunshine, could you get that?" Shaw didn't shift his attention from Pete Cypher.

Sunshine peered at him over the top of her book. "You've got two legs and two hands."

"I can't," Shaw whined. "I've invested forty-five minutes in this. You've read that book three times. Okay? Please?"

Sunshine sighed, pulled herself up, and trudged to the door.

"Hello, my name is Jessica Mordente. I'm a reporter with the *Los Angeles Times*," Shaw heard a woman say. "Is Sergeant Shaw in?"

Shaw groaned. Cypher squinted at the three Ninjas and pointed his digital wristwatch at them.

"Come in, Ms. Mordente," Sunshine said.

"Thank you," Mordente replied.

Shaw reluctantly rose from the couch, his eyes on the set, and back stepped toward the door. *What has Cypher got in his watch?*

"Ronny!" Sunshine shouted.

Shaw whirled around, startled, and flashed an apologetic smile at Sunshine and Mordente.

"Sergeant Shaw?" Mordente ventured, offering her hand to him.

"Yes," Shaw replied, a questioning look on his face, and shook Mordente's hand. "What can I do for you, Ms. Mordente?"

"Please, call me Jessie. Everyone does."

"Right," Shaw said, leading Mordente to the couch. He stopped to watch a pin-size missile blast out of Cypher's watch and zoom toward the terrified Ninjas.

"Ronny, why don't you turn off the TV so we can talk?" Sunshine urged. Shaw reluctantly switched off the set and sat on the arm of the couch beside Mordente.

"So, what's your story?" Shaw asked glumly.

"Mr. Jury." Mordente replied.

Shaw felt the anxiety flare in his chest and shrugged, as if her remark meant nothing to him. "Well, I could have saved you a trip," he casually remarked. "It's an ongoing investigation, and I can't release any information."

Sunshine shot a curious look at Shaw as she picked a discarded pair of her wooden platform shoes off the living room floor.

"I think Mr. Jury is the man who foiled that bank robbery this afternoon," Mordente said.

So do I, Shaw thought. "You may be right, then again you may not. It's speculation at this point, and I'm in no position right now to discuss the case." Shaw narrowed his eyes and wondered what she was after. "Really, why don't you contact our press relations office in the morning? It's been a long day and—"

"Do you have any evidence in the Mr. Jury case?" she interrupted. "Any fingerprints, witnesses, suspects?"

"Look, I already told you. I can't discuss the case." A stroke of anger colored his voice. "We have leads we are actively pursuing."

"That's the same speech Stocker used to give me back when he was chief of police," she commented dryly. "C'mon, Sergeant, hasn't anything changed since then?"

Shaw didn't like the way this conversation was going. He felt as though his words were footsteps in a mine field. "That's all I can tell you. I don't want to risk jeopardizing the investigation. You already know what I'm authorized to tell you. The only description we have is from a cashier in a Quick Stop market. He says Mr. Jury is a short Oriental with a weight problem."

"Sergeant, you once arrested Brett Macklin because you thought he was Mr. Jury," she said evenly. "Isn't that true?"

Sunshine came beside Shaw and wrapped her arm around his waist.

"Not exactly," Shaw said, wishing he had Cypher's watch right now. "But we *did* bring him in for questioning." Shaw's heart pounded. She couldn't know the truth, could she? "Just what are you getti—"

"Why did you arrest him?" she interjected pointedly, her words coming in a rush. "What evidence did you have linking him to the murders? Was it simply his revenge motive or something more that led you to arrest him? Is he still a suspect?"

Shaw stood up, strode silently to the front door, and held it open. "Ms. Mordente, that's enough for tonight. You want to interview me, you call the press information office in the morning and we'll go from there."

Mordente scratched her cheek and smiled. "What are you afraid of, Sergeant?"

"I'm afraid you're not going to leave and the whole evening will be shot to hell."

She stood up and shifted her gaze between Sunshine and Shaw. "You have been friends with Brett Macklin for a long time. I think if he was Mr. Jury, you might be tempted to cover up for him."

"Stop playing games with us," Sunshine shot back. "You're saying Mack is Mr. Jury and you're accusing Ronny of covering for him."

"Mack and I are close friends, Ms. Mordente," Shaw said. "I'd be lying if I said it wasn't painful having to question him about the Mr. Jury killings. But you're right. He had motive." Shaw leaned against the wall. "The fact is, Brett Macklin is a man who has had to endure a lot of personal tragedy lately. Someone out there got mad about that and decided to do something about it."

"How do you know that someone isn't your friend? It's the logical assumption, Sergeant."

"Ms. Mordente, I'd like to watch a little TV, make some popcorn, spend a quiet evening at home, okay?" Shaw tilted his head toward the door. "Let's call it a night."

Mordente acquiesced. "All right." She pulled a card out of her skirt pocket and gave it to Shaw. "Here's my card if you want to reach me." Mordente glanced at Sunshine. "Thank you both for your time."

Shaw closed the door behind Mordente and tore up the card into scraps. *It's finally happening*, he thought, *what I knew would happen all along.* He felt a chill ride over him, raising goosebumps on his flesh and making him shiver.

He walked into the living room and stood beside the fire, the heat warming his back. The heat against his back only made the iciness over the rest of his body more acute. *Someone is picking apart our flimsy cover-up*, he warned himself. *It's only a matter of time now before the whole thing comes crumbling down and crushes us all.* He recognized his chills for what they were—the same chills he felt as a child whenever the doctor wanted to give him a blood test or throat culture. The chills of unadulterated fear.

Sunshine crossed her legs and sat down in front of him. "I hate to admit it, Ronny, but she has a point."

Shaw tossed the bits of paper into the fire and sat down on the couch behind her. He willed the fear out of his voice. "Sure she does. That doesn't make it the truth."

"But it *is* the truth, isn't it?" she asked softly, staring into the fire.

"No," he told her quietly, one last lie in the whole string of lies that he felt, with aching certainty, would soon become his noose.

Luck didn't seem to be on Mort Suderson's side Friday night. His windbreaker wouldn't zip up, and there was no dry place to squat on the roof of the building across from Orlock's warehouse.

Sitting on the roof was like wading in a stagnant pond. A vast puddle of rainwater stretched across the roof, reaching into all the corners that afforded the best view of the street below.

LEE GOLDBERG

There was no way around it. Mort had to get wet. His socks were soaked sponges inside his wet tennis shoes and made his feet feel like solid blocks of ice.

Mort sniffled and wiped his nose with the back of his hand. He cursed himself for not bringing his heavy Levi jacket. He squatted in the far left-hand corner of the warehouse roofline, two stories above the street, Orlock's warehouse in front of him an alley to his left. The last, dimming rays of the sun gave the greenish haze above the city a sickly glow. It reminded Mort that the poison air didn't disappear at night—it simply hid in the darkness.

He glanced at his watch. It was 6:30 P.M. Perfect, he thought. He wanted to settle in early.

The gun was felt snug against him in his LAPD-issue shoulder holster, and the Canon AE-1 hung around his neck. With nothing else to do, he decided to play with the camera. He sighted Orlock's warehouse through the viewfinder, adjusting the zoom lens. If he wanted to, he knew he could snap clear pictures of the bolts on the steel warehouse door.

This is going to be easy, Mort thought.

He aimed the camera at the moon, playfully thinking he'd take a few pictures of craters.

Mort heard something splash in the water behind him. He lowered the camera and jerked his head around. His eyes caught the flash of steel an instant too late. The wrench slammed into the side of his head, and a blinding burst of intense pain consumed him. In the fraction of a second before darkness swallowed his thoughts, Mort realized he should have guessed there would be others who wanted to settle in early.

Tice wiped the blood off the wrench with a white handkerchief and slipped them both into the pocket of his overcoat. He examined his black-gloved hands to see if any blood had splattered them. They were clean. His thin lips stretched into a self-satisfied grin as he casually glanced down at Mort, who lay at his feet wide-eyed but unseeing, tiny rivulets of blood crawling down his cheek.

Tice lifted Mort by the armpits and dragged him through the water to the building's edge. Then, with the heel of his black shoes, he pushed Mort over the edge with a sharp kick.

Mort's body fell silently, landing in the trashbin in the alley below with a dull thud.

Brett Macklin parked the Impala across from Orlock's warehouse thirty minutes later and immediately noticed the thin, long-legged man in the black overcoat standing out front.

Macklin switched off the ignition and stared at the man. The guy gave Macklin a bad feeling in his gut. Macklin thought the man could make a good living playing Gestapo agents in low-budget World War II movies. That thought didn't do much to quell Macklin's uneasiness.

Thank God there's someone with a gun watching out for me, Macklin thought. He opened the car door and walked casually toward Orlock's warehouse. As Macklin neared, he could see a tight grin on the man's face.

"Mr. Smith?" the man hissed, approaching Macklin.

Macklin recognized the voice. It was Tice, the man who had answered Orlock's phone.

"Yeah," Macklin said.

Tice suddenly drove his fist hard into Macklin's stomach, catching Macklin completely by surprise. Macklin choked forward, gagging, the air forced out of his lungs. Tice stepped close to Macklin, who was hunched over and gasping for air, and grabbed a handful of Macklin's hair. Steadying Macklin's head, Tice rammed his knee into Macklin's neck and released him.

Macklin tumbled backward and lay inert on the pavement, wheezing and skirting the boundaries of consciousness. He was completely paralyzed with pain, sapped of the air necessary to move. Yet he was aware of Tice bending over, opening his flight jacket, and removing his .357 Magnum.

A long white Lincoln limousine snaked around the warehouse and slid to a stop in front of them. Tice grabbed Macklin by the collar and lifted him up, slamming him back against the warehouse wall. Macklin blinked open his eyes and saw the tinted rear window of the limousine slide down.

A man with heavy purple lips sneered at him from inside the car. The skin on the man's face was pale, stretched tight over his skull and hugging the sunken contours of his cheeks and the broad ridge of his brow.

"No one treats me like a common thug, Mr. Smith," Orlock said. "You're a stupid man. A dead man."

C'mon, Mort, Macklin thought, come save me from this. "Aren't you forgetting something?" Macklin coughed out between labored breaths. He was a rag doll in Tice's hands. "Kill me, and your picture goes to the DA and the press."

Orlock shrugged carelessly. "I'll take that chance."

Macklin hadn't counted on that at all.

"Good night." Orlock waved at him and then leaned back in his seat, disappearing from view. The window hummed closed and the limousine moved away slowly. The warehouse door opened. Tice yanked Macklin forward, twisted his right arm painfully behind his back, and led him toward the doorway.

Macklin glanced at the warehouse across the street. *Mort, where the fuck are you?*

"Your friend has taken the night off," Tice grinned as if he had read Macklin's thoughts. Tice's words struck Macklin like a blow.

Ahead, Macklin saw Wesley Saputo standing in the doorway. Macklin could see Orlock's van parked beside Saputo and the plywood, plank-supported back sides of movie sets in the center of the warehouse.

"Mr. Smith," Saputo said, "you are going to be a movie star."

"I am?" Macklin sputtered. "A romance? A light comedy, perhaps?"

Saputo stepped back and let Tice and Macklin edge past him. "No," Saputo laughed. "A snuff film."

CHAPTER TEN

M acklin stumbled over a confusing latticework of electrical cables that criss-crossed the expanse of the huge warehouse as Tice urged him forward toward the sets. Large, standing movie lights bathed the center of the warehouse hot white.

His eyes followed the cables from the lights to a battered junction box, held together with electrical tape, on the floor to his left. Beyond it, in the far corner of the warehouse, Macklin could see stacks of film canisters, bottles of thinner, and gallons of paint.

"Move, Mr. Smith," Tice growled, and wrenched up Mackline's arm. Macklin winced at the sharp pain, his tendons threatening to snap like taut rubber bands.

Macklin stumbled clumsily alongside Tice. Saputo and two of the gorillas Macklin had seen when he had staked out the warehouse fell into step beside them.

They weaved through several standing movie sets—a kitchen, a doctor's office, and a classroom—to a dining room. A birthday cake sat on the table amidst party favors and balloons. Two of Saputo's crewmen stood on ladders adjusting lights while Lyle Franken put a canister of film into the movie camera.

Macklin saw a little girl wearing a pink-and-white-checked gingham dress sitting at the end of the table, her tear-streaked face drooping with sadness, a red-striped cone-shaped party hat askew on her head. A cardboard cake covered with unlit candles sat in the middle of the table, surrounded by gifts and party favors. A blond-haired boy, who Macklin guessed was perhaps ten years old, was wearing black bikini briefs and playing with a half-dozen Hot Wheels toy cars in one corner of the set.

"Hey, who is this? What's going on?" whined a heavyset man with a thick moustache. Standing beside him was a gangly woman in gray leather pants and a pink Camp Beverly Hills sweatshirt, a cigarette stub dangling out from under her upper lip.

Saputo smiled. "Mr. Smith here is the star of our next picture."

"Can you fit our son Jimmy into it?" the woman asked, her cigarette bobbing. Macklin saw the boy raise his head at the mention of his name.

"I don't think so." Saputo grinned at Macklin, as if the two were sharing in a friendly, secret joke.

"We could use the extra money," the father said. "The kid has been a pain in the ass for ten years."

"Ten years and nine months," the mother added with a grimace.

Macklin narrowed his eyes at the boy's parents. "How can you do this to your son?"

"I didn't make society sick, okay?" The woman waved her finger reproachfully at Macklin. "I don't know who the fuck you are, but I'll tell you this—if the pervs get off looking at my kid's picture, I'd rather they do that than go and rape someone, you know?"

"You're doing it for the money. You don't care about anything else," Macklin replied.

"Hey, the kid knows what he's doing. I asked him if he wanted to be in the movies and he said he did." The father cocked his head toward the set and yelled to his son out of the corner of his mouth. "Right, Jimmy?"

"Sure, Dad," the boy mumbled, absorbed in his toy cars again.

"So the kid helps Mom and Dad bring home the bacon." Saputo grinned. "I call that wholesome family unity."

"You're scum," Macklin hissed.

"And you're on borrowed time." Saputo motioned to Tice. "Take this man to the dungeon."

Macklin shot a sideways glance at Tice. "He's little heavy on the melodrama, don't you think?"

Tice shoved Macklin ahead to the next set, which was designed to look like a medieval torture chamber. Macklin arched his eyebrows in surprise. A makeshift wooden rack rested beside a backdrop painted to look like it was made of stone. Cuffed chains dangled from the wall. Macklin saw a mace, the weapon consisting of a spiked iron ball and chain, and a branding iron lying on the floor.

"You guys have got to be kidding," Macklin remarked with a cynical grin.

Tice whipped the wrench out of his pocket and slapped Macklin viciously across the face with it. As Macklin fell to the floor, the warehouse swirling around him in a painful blur, he realized they weren't.

"I thought Mr. Jury was a fat Oriental midget." Jackie Laylor scratched her cleavage and fingered the cursor controls on her computer terminal, the story on the screen reflecting off her sunglasses.

She didn't like computers. She remembered her mother telling her that sitting too close to the TV would make her uterus shrivel up and her father's warning that invisible rays coming off the screen would make her blind. A computer was just a TV with a keyboard to her. So she wore sunglasses to protect her eyes. And while other writers put the keyboard on their lap, she kept hers on the desk, far away from her uterus.

Jessica Mordente stood behind Laylor, looking over her shoulder as the city editor scanned Mordente's lengthy Mr. Jury article. She was certain Laylor had scratched cleavage to draw attention to those big breasts, as if to say to Mordente, "I've got it and you don't, baby."

"Jackie, forget that description of Mr. Jury," Mordente said wearily. "The kid at the Seven-Eleven or whatever is lying."

"What are you now, Jessie? Psychic?" Laylor sighed, scrolling through the story, the lighted characters rapidly passing across the screen. "Look, I can't print this."

"What do you mean? What's wrong?" Mordente tried to keep her voice even, keep her anger in check. She had spent the last two hours cleaning up her rough draft and inserting Shaw's vague remarks. She wanted the story to make the Sunday Metro section, maybe even the front page. "It's great stuff. We're telling the city who their mysterious vigilante is."

"We are, huh?" Laylor stored the article with a few quick keystrokes. The eighty-five column inches blinked off the screen. She took off her sunglasses and rubbed her tired, bloodshot brown eyes. "This story is no story."

Mordente stepped back, stunned and outraged. "I don't follow. I've tracked down Mr. Jury, exposed him, and you're telling me there is no story."

Laylor sighed. "You got the last part right. There may be a story later, but not now. What you've got here, if we were irresponsible enough to publish it, is the grounds for a multimillion-dollar libel suit. Brett Macklin would own the *Los Angeles Times* after he got through with us."

"Brett Macklin *is* Mr. Jury. It's all there. His father was killed by the Bounty Hunters gang and," Mordente snapped her fingers "bang, they were all killed by Mr. Jury."

"Coincidence, Jessie," Laylor responded. "C'mon, you're a better reporter than that. You have no facts, just a lot of iffy circumstantial evidence."

"Okay, here's a fact. Two detectives are assigned to the Mr. Jury case. One disappears and the other, surprise of surprises, is Sergeant Ronald Shaw, Macklin's oldest friend."

"So? Maybe putting Shaw on the case wasn't the wisest decision the LAPD ever made, but it still doesn't prove anything." Laylor shrugged. "You're reaching."

"Jackie! Don't you see?" Mordente yelled. "Can't you smell it? This guy Macklin has blood on his hands. One cop realized that and arrested Macklin for murder. Don't you find it odd that Macklin was released the next day?"

"He was innocent—how's that for an explanation?"

Mordente went on, undaunted. "Then the arresting officer disappears. Now someone plants a bomb in Macklin's car and kills his girlfriend. Mystery, coincidence, and crime sure seem attracted to Macklin."

"You said it. Maybe he's just had his share of rotten luck. Maybe he *is* a shaky character. That doesn't make him Mr. Jury." The city editor rose from her seat, noticing for the first time that their argument had caught the attention of the newsroom staff. A half-dozen heads were turned in their direction. "Face it, there isn't anything to the story yet. If you can dig up something more, something solid, I'll run with it. Not yet."

"This man can't be the innocent bystander he says he is!"

"He sure can, Jessie," she replied evenly, quietly, hoping Mordente would follow her cue and settle down. "Until someone *proves* otherwise."

"I have! The story is there," Mordente roared. "Or have you been sitting behind a desk too long to know a story when it bites you in the ass?"

Laylor stiffened. Anyone who hadn't been watching them before certainly was now. "I'm going to write that remark off as exhaustion. I've been working you real hard. That had better be why you've suddenly reverted to a cub reporter with dreams of front page, banner headlines, because I'm giving you three days off and you had better come back the reliable reporter you used to be."

Mordente's face reddened with anger and, as she felt the stares of her coworkers, a trace of embarrassment as well. "Jackie, listen to me. I'm convinced Brett Macklin, alias Mr. Jury, walked into the bank robbery yesterday afternoon. If we run with the story, that will pressure the police into comparing the bullets in the bankrobbers' bodies with those from Mr. Jury's other victims."

"Don't make me get any harsher, Jessie. The answer is no."

"I'm working an FBI source now," Mordente said sharply. "If Macklin is in the photos the bank camera took, then we've got Mr. Jury."

Laylor walked away. "No."

Mordente wanted to scream furiously at the top of her lungs. Instead, her body seemed to tremble for a moment before she willed herself to turn away and walk back to her desk. She picked up the phone and dialed.

"Hello, Chet? This is Jessie." She tapped her pencil against the VDT screen. "Why don't we get together for dinner? Yeah, Sunday is fine for me. See you then."

The mental disarray of returning consciousness was becoming a familiar state to Brett Macklin. Before his father's murder, his only experience with unconsciousness had been a fastball to the head in high school. Nowadays it seemed like everyone was trying to pitch something against his head. The whirling kaleidoscope of sensory perceptions, like a blurry television picture that defies adjustment, didn't make Macklin as insecure as it used to. He no longer grasped for solid bits of perception, but rather waited for the storm to abate.

After a few minutes, things inside his head began to settle and Macklin tried to blink open his eyes, which felt weighed down with cement blocks. Mucus gave his throat a sticky, acidic feel, and swallowing burned. His heartbeat pounded in his head and his appendages tingled as if they were asleep.

Macklin focused his eyes on the rafters on the ceiling above him and realized he was lying flat on his back. His arms were stretched out behind him. He tried to lower them to his sides and felt a bolt of pain race through his body.

What the fuck?

Macklin peering down at his feet and saw his ankles were tied with rope. He guessed the rest. He was on the rack, ropes tied around his wrists and ankles, pulling them taut. Macklin knew all it would take was a crank or two on the pulleys at his feet and behind his head and *wrip!*, his guts would slop onto the floor like a plate of spaghetti absently knocked off the dinner table. Macklin closed his eyes and tried to think.

This is one film Macky boy won't be able to stomach. Stomach HAHAHAHAHA! teased a devilish voice inside him. *Hey, Macky, Gene Shalit says you'll bust a gut laughing at this madcap comedy HAHAHAHA!*

I'm going to get out of this, Macklin told himself.

"How are you doing, Mr. Smith?" Macklin heard Wesley Saputo say, smelling the nicotine breath before Saputo appeared over him. "Are you ready to become a star?"

"You're a real tough guy, Saputo, a real specimen of manhood. You tie *me* down and then slither around molesting defenseless *children,*" Macklin said. "You're some kind of stud, all right. Next you're gonna start fucking corpses."

Saputo's face flushed with anger. "As an actor, Mr. *Macklin,* you'll need to stretch a bit for *this* role." Saputo leaned forward and turned the crank clockwise.

The pain clawed its way up Macklin's throat as a scream. He gritted his teeth and forced it back.

"Relax, Macklin, you won't have long to wait." Saputo walked away. "Your screen debut is imminent."

Macklin lay panting, his body drenched with sweat, the pain ebbing into an intense ache. He closed his eyes and enjoyed the pain-killing, cool darkness. Time slipped past him until he heard a voice.

"What are you doing, mister?" a meek voice inquired.

He turned his head and saw the little girl bashfully standing a safe two feet away. Macklin blinked his eyes clear, not knowing how long he had been blacked out. The girl had chocolate cake smeared around her face.

"Come here, honey," Macklin whispered gently.

She stepped back. Macklin realized his tactic was all wrong. Everyone was probably talking sweetly and quietly to her, gaining her reluctant trust and then doing her harm.

"What's your name?" Macklin asked in his normal voice.

"Erica Tandy. I'm ten."

"Really? Is it your birthday today?" Macklin wanted to order her to untie his bonds, but his rational side realized the necessity of moving slowly. Painfully slowly.

"No." She stepped toward him. "They're making me pretend."

"Where's your mom and dad?"

She shrugged. "I want to go home."

Macklin felt her sadness and wanted to reach out and comfort her. He imagined Cory, his daughter, the loss and fear she would feel if she were in Erica's place. "I do too. If you come here and help me untie these ropes, we can leave here. Would you like that?"

"Uh-huh," she mumbled.

"Come here." He jerked his head back, motioning to her. She took a step forward.

"ERICA!" Saputo yelled from behind the set. Erica froze. "Beautiful? Come here!"

Erica shot Macklin one frightened glance and then dashed back behind the wall to the dining room set. Macklin dropped his head and closed his eyes. *Damn!*

CHAPTER ELEVEN

The Cadillac exploded again and again in Macklin's mind. It was a relentless pounding that rocked his body and sent shock waves of pain rolling through him.

Macklin squeezed his eyes shut, willing away the torturous images. A giant tombstone loomed up in his psyche. Six names were carved into it.

J. D. Macklin. Melody. Saul. Moe. Cheshire. *Mort.*

There was no way back now. There had been an irrevocable, jarring turn in the course of Macklin's life and the bodies of his loved ones lined the curve.

Dad, Melody, Saul, Moe, Cheshire... Mort.

The only name missing was his own.

"Help me, mister," Macklin heard Erica whimper. He flashed open his eyes and saw her standing beside him again, naked, tears rolling down her puffy cheeks.

"Erica," Macklin whispered. "I want you to turn that handle behind me counterclockwise. Do you know what that means?"

She nodded.

"Okay, go ahead. Do it slowly." She reached out to the handle and pushed it down. Immediately, Macklin felt the muscles in his arms recoiling painfully. "A little more, Erica."

She pulled the crank around to an upright position. That gave Macklin enough slack to sit up. He felt a hot flush burn his skin as blood surged through his body, revitalizing his traumatized limbs. Macklin quickly began to untie the knots around his wrists.

"Where's Erica?" Saputo yelled from behind the set. Macklin saw Erica tremble. Erica wasn't going to go back to that set. Which meant, Macklin knew, that Saputo would come looking for her. Macklin freed one wrist and struggled with the rope on the other.

"Damnit! Who let her wander away?" Saputo growled. "Earl, go find her. She's got to get back here. We've still got to do the come shot."

Macklin leaned forward and frantically pulled on the rope around his ankles, trying to loosen it enough to get free. Erica whimpered.

"Shhhhh," Macklin hissed at her. He heard heavy footsteps approaching.

Macklin freed one ankle. The footsteps were close, a yard or two away.

"Run!" Macklin whispered to Erica and fell back on the rack, extending his arms as if he were bound. With his left hand, he felt around for the mace.

Erica froze.

"Run, Erica!" Macklin's hand found the mace. He hid his hand behind the pulley as Earl, one of Saputo's gorillas, emerged to Macklin's right.

"Hey, kid, get away from him!" Earl roared. With both hands he pushed Erica aside. She shrieked and fell to the floor, scrambling away like a frightened animal.

Earl laughed, watching her bare rear end disappear behind the wall. "The little runt," he mumbled, turning his head and looking down at Macklin. In the instant it took Earl to comprehend the meaning of Macklin's loosened bonds, Macklin swung the mace, the thorny iron ball whipping into Earl's startled face.

The mace audibly smacked into Earl's skull, the spikes plunging deep into his eyeball, temple, and cheek. Earl screamed and blindly stumbled back, the mace stuck in his head, blood gushing out of his face. Macklin yanked the rope off his ankle, leaped off the rack, and pulled the gun out of Earl's shoulder holster.

Macklin shoved the gun barrel into Earl's fleshy stomach and squeezed the trigger. The blast of the .38 shook the warehouse. Earl burst apart like a *piñata,* splashing blood against the dungeon wall.

"Get the kids out of the way. Lock 'em in the van," Macklin heard Saputo shout. Macklin scrambled through a maze of sets toward the opposite end of the warehouse.

Saputo called out after him. "Forget it, Macklin! There are no windows and no other doors. There's only one way out of here for you, asshole!"

Macklin crouched behind the last set and peered around the edge. He saw a stack of tires against the wall to his left, by the breaker box. Ahead and to his right were the film and the painting supplies he had seen when he came in. He glanced at the octuple arms of electrical cord that stretched out from the junction box on the slick cement floor. Scanning the ceiling, he saw only sprinkler heads. Not a single skylight. Saputo was right. He was trapped.

Macklin sprinted across the open floor toward the paint supplies, hoping there might be something there that could help him escape. The sound of a footfall behind him made him jerk around midstep. He saw a man and muzzle flash when the floor suddenly slipped out from under him, the gun's report cracking in his ear. As he hit the floor on his right shoulder, he sensed the bullet streaking above his head and realized he had tripped over the junction box.

Macklin bolted upright and fired. The slug slammed into the gunman's chest and kicked him back into a set wall. The line of sets tumbled down like a row of dominoes.

Macklin scrambled to his feet and, glancing over his shoulder, saw paint thinner spilling out of a jug that had apparently been pierced by the gunman's bullet.

There *is* a way out, Macklin thought. Quickly, Macklin searched through the gunman's bloody clothes, turning out the pockets. *C'mon, let it be there* …. The gunman shook spasmodically as death tightened its grip on him. Macklin looked into the gunman's open, blank eyes and felt the pack of matches in the man's inside jacket pocket. *Bingo!*

"There he is!" the father cried out, appearing around the edge of the fallen sets, waving his finger at Macklin.

Macklin struck a match and lit the matchbook. Saputo and Franken, brandishing snub-nosed revolvers, and two of Saputo's crewmen emerged behind Macklin, who tossed the flaming matchbook into the stream of developer fluid and dived away.

"Hit the deck!" Saputo screamed, throwing himself forward.

The fire chased the fluid back into the jug. The jug exploded, splattering flame out in all directions. Macklin crawled toward the opposite wall. The blaze spread in an instant, feeding on the nearby packs of film.

Glancing back, Macklin saw the flames climb the wall, licking the ceiling and prompting the sprinklers to life. Macklin tipped over the stack of tires and threw himself on them just as the water rained down.

Macklin aimed his gun at the junction box on the watery floor and saw Saputo and his men rise to their feet.

Saputo grinned at Macklin and pointed his gun at him. "You're mine, Macklin," he yelled over the roaring blaze and cool shower.

Macklin fired, splitting open the junction box and exposing it to the water. He heard the whiplike snap of electric current. The movie lights fluttered.

Saputo's eyes flashed open wide in an instant of terror and surprise. His body twitched and convulsed, hundreds of volts riding through him and bouncing him up and down like a human pogo stick.

Macklin, insulated by the tires, stared transfixed at Saputo and his men jerked obscenely across the floor in a last dance of death. He reached up to the breaker box and switched off the electricity. The warehouse, lit by the flickering of the dying flames, smelled like ammonia and spoiled meat.

He stood up and ran along the wall to the van. The mother's corpse lay twisted in a puddle beside the movie camera, her red tongue lolling out of her open mouth. Macklin stepped over her body and splashed through the water to the van. He put his gun into his waistband and pounded a fist against the side of the van.

"Are you okay in there?" he shouted, hoping the van's tires had kept them safe from the electric current.

"Uh-huh," Erica and Jimmy mumbled in unison from inside the van.

"Stay put. Help is on the way." Macklin, soaking wet, flung open the warehouse door.

Tice stood outside in the alleyway in front of him, a laconic grin on his face and Macklin's .357 Magnum in his hand.

"Help is here," Tice whispered. Macklin saw Tice's finger tighten on the trigger and braced himself for the bullet that would rip through his stomach. Macklin winced, the handgun's deafening report ringing out twice in his ears. Macklin stiffened. And felt nothing.

He tentatively opened his eyes and saw Tice sprawled on the ground, blood frothing out of a ragged crater in his head. Chunks of blood-soaked gray-beige brain matter and jagged slivers of bone dripped onto the pavement. Macklin took in a deep breath and looked up and down the street, confused. There was no one in sight.

Then he heard the sound of someone gagging in the alley beside the warehouse across the street. Macklin sprinted to the other side of the street and moved cautiously into the alley.

He stopped short, stunned. Mort leaned over the side of the trashbin vomiting into the street.

"Mort, you're alive!" Macklin said with astonishment.

"I sure as hell don't feel like it," Mort groaned, holding the gun limply in his right hand. Mort steadied himself with his left hand and lifted a leg over the rim. Macklin wrapped his arms around Mort's waist and helped him out.

"You saved my life, Mort. Thanks."

"No problem. Anytime." Mort heaved for breath, dizzy, the sour taste of vomit in his mouth and nose.

"Take it easy." Macklin put his arm around Mort and held him tightly. He noticed the matted hair and dried blood on the side of Mort's head. "What happened to you?"

Mort swallowed and glanced up. The white oval moon shone down on him and he could see the side of the warehouse he had been atop. The pieces fell together for him.

"That asshole I shot must've sidelined me with a crowbar or something, I dunno," Mort shivered. "I guess he tossed me off the building. That garbage bin must be the only thing that saved me from being a nasty smudge on the pavement. The way my head and stomach feel, I think I would rather have died. Damn concussion."

Mort stiffened. Bile shot up his throat, spurting out and onto the ground in one quick convulsion. "Fuck…"

Macklin could hear the sound of police sirens drawing near. "Are you okay? Can you walk?"

Mort nodded. "Yeah, let's go."

As Macklin led Mort to his car, he realized his anger would never die. It wasn't the Bounty Hunter gang or Wesley Saputo or Crocker Orlock. They were just germs, part of a bigger disease that was growing and infecting the vital organs of society. He hadn't stopped it when he avenged his father's death. And, Macklin knew, it wouldn't stop if Orlock's operation was crushed, either.

No more of my friends will die. I won't let the disease spread. The voice inside Macklin that cried for retribution was now his own.

Mr. Jury and Brett Macklin were one.

CHAPTER TWELVE

"Mister Jury is dead."

Mayor Jed Stocker solemnly faced the two dozen reporters in the press room and reveled in the absolute attention his statement engendered.

Stocker stood crisp and clean in a dark blue pinstriped suit under the city's seal, doing his best to exude leadership and stature. This was the first time he had ever shut the reporters up, and on a slow news day like Saturday, Stocker was sure this press conference would dominate the local media, just as he had planned.

Jessica Mordente's perplexed expression didn't escape Stocker's notice. First of all, as his pick as the best-looking of the LA press corps, he was always looking at her. Secondly, that's the reaction he had intended to evoke. She was, no surprise to him, the first to break the stunned silence.

"Who is he?" she asked.

Stocker shrugged. "We don't know. He was found with a bullet in his head outside a Culver City warehouse."

"How do you know it's Mr. Jury?" Mordente, Stocker thought, had the look of a shell-shocked soldier.

"A good guess." Stocker grinned. "He was carrying a .357 Magnum that ballistics testing has conclusively tied to the Mr. Jury killings." He leaned forward against the wooden podium. "Police investigation thus far suggests that Mr. Jury was on the trail of a gang of child pornographers who used the warehouse to film motion pictures that featured kidnapped young children."

Stocker cleared his throat. "These children were taken accidentally and murdered. Mr. Jury killed the gang involved and rescued two children, one of whom was Erica Tandy, the ten-year-old girl who disappeared yesterday while playing at a Van Nuys park."

"What happened to Mr. Jury?" Al Zimmer, a reporter with the *Herald-Examiner*, slurped up the saliva dribbling out the corner of his mouth. Zimmer's chin was always set with the spittle forced between his lips by the ever-present wad of chewing gum.

"We aren't sure." Stocker sighed. "He was fatally wounded in the head by someone outside. Perhaps one of the gang escaped. We don't know."

"What do the children say?" A toupé-topped TV reporter cried out from the back of the room.

"They are severely traumatized, as you can well imagine. Erica is under a doctor's supervision and remembers nothing at this time." Stocker shifted his weight uncomfortably. "The other child, a young boy, has a long history as a victim of sexual molestation. Sergeant Clive Barer of our Sexually Exploited Child Unit is handling the investigation."

Mordente frowned, narrowing her eyes. "Who was Mr. Jury?" she asked again, noticeably dissatisfied with what she was hearing.

"We don't know."

"Of course you don't," Mordente mumbled angrily, and folded her arms under her chest.

"We have tried everything—dental charts, fingerprints, the works," Stocker argued. "Still we come up blank. This man lived and died an enigma." Stocker hurriedly shuffled together the papers on the podium. "That's all for now. We'll let you know as soon as more information becomes available."

The mayor walked away, dodging a volley of questions, and slipped out a side door and into a narrow gray corridor. Shaw leaned against the wall, his hands in the pockets of his jeans.

"Did Mordente buy it?" Shaw asked.

Stocker smiled, clapping his hand on Shaw's shoulder. "Our worries are over. The dogs have been thrown off the scent."

Brett Macklin lay in the bathtub, his knees bent out of the water and his head propped up by an inflated plastic pillow stuck to the tile wall. Steamy water dribbled out of the spigot in a weak and steady stream, keeping the bath water hot and soothing.

He absently stroked the rim of a chilly wineglass, half filled with Chablis, that rested on the lint-dotted red bathmat and listened to Stevie Nicks crooning gently from the bedroom.

His muscles were relaxed for the first time in days. Tension floated out of him and the world began to seem less black, less ominous, to him. Droplets of perspiration dotted his face.

His watch, on the floor beside the glass, beeped once, letting him know it was noon and his bath would be short-lived.

As if on the cue, the phone, which Macklin had brought into the bathroom and set on the toilet seat, rang shrilly, shattering his calm. Sitting up, he reached out for it and extended his legs in the hot water. The tortured muscles, so brutally stretched by the rack, said "ahhhhhhhhhhhhhh" to him.

"Hello," Macklin drawled sleepily.

"It's me," Shaw replied briskly. "The press conference went smoothly. Mr. Jury is dead, at least as far as the press is concerned."

"Good," Macklin said. "What about Orlock?"

"We've turned up reels of kiddie porn and hundreds of mailing lists at the warehouse," he replied. "His kiddie porn operation is over and we're moving in on dozens of his friends. Christ, Mack, some of the names on his mailing list would shock you."

"So, you have Orlock behind bars, right?"

A heavy silence fell for a moment between them.

"Ronny, how can he still be a free man?" Macklin barked.

"The ties to Orlock are still tenuous," Shaw replied mutely, "obscured by layers of dummy corporations and other crap. His lawyers are holding us at bay, at least for now, fielding our questions and keeping Orlock out of it."

"I don't like this, Ron, not one damn bit."

"I know. Neither do I," Shaw said, pausing for a few seconds before speaking again. "I've contacted Judge Fitz and he's reviewing all the evidence we've got. He should have a decision by tomorrow morning. And Orlock is scared. I think he will run. Either way, this will break tomorrow."

"How are you coming on the equipment I asked you for last night?"

"We're getting it together, but it's not easy." Shaw sounded tired. "I'll probably be able to drop it off at your hangar sometime this evening."

"All right." Macklin turned the spigot knobs with his feet, shutting off the water. "Thanks, Ron."

"Don't thank me, Mack, thank the mayor." Shaw hung up, and Macklin put the reciever back on the cradle. The doorbell chimed downstairs.

Macklin groaned. It never rains, it just storms.

The doorbell chimed again.

"Coming!" Macklin yelled. He pulled out the stopper with his foot, letting let the water drain out, stood up dripping, and reached for his yellow terry-cloth bathrobe.

"Hold on!" He scampered out of the bathroom and down the stairs to the front door, beads of sweat rolling down his face, his damp body clinging to the robe.

Wiping the sweat out of his eye, Macklin opened the door. Jessica Mordente stood on the porch. He noticed now, in the sunlight, the dark-skinned sensuality and sharp features he hadn't seen a few nights earlier. Her loose-fitting white blouse, trim khaki pants, and matching low-heeled boots accentuated her slender build.

"Oh, I'm sorry," she said, eyeing Macklin from head to toe. She too liked what she saw. "I didn't mean to disturb you."

Macklin shrugged. *So Mr. Jury is dead, huh? Somebody forgot to tell her.* "What do you want?"

"To apologize," she ventured softly. Macklin raised an eyebrow, relieved but wary. "I was trying to find Mr. Jury. I investigated the whole thing very hard, very seriously. My strident style isn't always the most diplomatic. The police found him today, dead." She shrugged apologetically. "I'm sorry if I treated you rudely, Mr. Macklin."

Macklin smiled, not sure whether he believed her. "It's okay. I didn't exactly give you the VIP treatment either." Her eyes drew him in. Words spilled out of him before he knew it. "Look, ah, I was just getting dressed. Why don't you come in for a moment, have a cup of coffee, we'll start off fresh."

Her eyes lit up. "I'd like that."

Macklin moved aside. *Shit, what am I getting myself into?* "Come in then, make yourself at home while I get ready." She walked past him and he closed the door.

"Have you ever been up in a helicopter?" he asked.

"No," she replied.

"Tell you what, then." Macklin led Mordente into the living room. "Why don't you go into the kitchen, rummage around, throw some things into the basket above the fridge, and we'll go on a helicopter ride around the city."

She laughed. "Sounds great to me."

"Then it's a date." Macklin patted her on the back and dashed up the stairs. She watched him go, and her smile faded. Half of her was excited. The other half was scared shitless.

They flew north over the beaches, following the Pacific Coast Highway, and then veered eastward over the wooded Palisades. The asphalt of Sunset Boulevard wound snakelike through the hills, forming the northern boundary of Brentwood, the upper-middle class neighborhood flanked on the south by San Vicente Boulevard.

Macklin glanced at Mordente and pointed out the stately houses that lined San Vicente.

"Those are houses that want to grow up and be mansions," he observed. "And look at that median strip. It's better landscaped than most of those homes."

She nodded, grinning. She noticed that a steady stream of joggers, in their designer warm-up suits and slashed sweatshirts and satin shorts, were scurrying up and down the grassy median. The joggers, to Mordente, seemed less interested in losing pounds and staying fit than in picking up bedmates.

"I can't believe how much you can see from up here," Mordente yelled into the mouthpiece of her headset.

Macklin winced, her booming in his ears. "You don't have to yell," he said softly, hoping to set an example. "I can hear you just fine."

She grimaced guiltily. "Sorry, it's just that I've never worn a spacesuit like this before."

Macklin nodded. "I know. You get used to the fireproof jumpsuits and all the paraphernalia after a while. Think of this as the Starship *Enterprise* on a strange new mission, and the get-up is easier to bear."

Mordente tossed back her head and laughed. "Actually, with these seat belts and the cozy back seat, I feel like I'm in a flying Buick LeSabre. All this needs is a hood ornament and a rear-view mirror with a garter on it or something."

"Sounds like you ride around in some classy cars, lady," Macklin joked, bringing the helicopter down low across the sprawling Veteran's Administration graveyard, the tombstones like neat rows of pebbles below them. He pulled the helicopter up again, over the UCLA dormitories, and then down over the track field.

"I spent hours down there." He pointed to the track. "That ground is soaked with my sweat."

"And I bet all the students think the bad smell in the air is from the smog."

Macklin chuckled dryly. "Cute. Anyway, I got into UCLA on a track scholarship. I thought I would be an Olympic athlete or something."

"What happened?"

He steered the helicopter slightly southward to a cluster of short gray buildings just shy of the mazelike structure of the medical center. "I got lost down there amidst the corridors of the engineering schools. Ended up at Hughes Aircraft boring myself to death."

"How did you escape?" she asked. Questions, Macklin thought, come very easy for her.

Macklin tapped the glass in front of him. "This baby. I decided I'd rather fly the aircraft than draw them all day."

He purposely made the turn northward sharp so Mordente was nearly passing over the ground sideways. Straightening the helicopter, Macklin turned to her and half smiled. "Airsick yet?"

"Nope." She grinned.

Macklin shook his head in mock disbelief. "Damn. That's the turn that gets them every time."

The trees that shrouded the elegant Bel Air homes of the stars and millionaires from the tour buses and casual passersby offered no protection from curious eyes in the sky. The homes were revealed in all their resplendent excess to Macklin and Mordente.

She whistled long. "If people only knew..."

"There would be an armed revolt," Macklin said, "starting with the poverty-stricken masses of Watts and sweeping through the rent-gouged apartment dwellers of the west side and Hollywood. The folks down there would have to dig moats around their castles."

"Castles is right," Mordente murmured, her face pressed to the glass, staring down in wonder at the vast acreage, the glimmering blue swimming pools, and the massive homes reminiscent of the seventeenth-century estates that dot the England countryside.

"There are some modern wonders, too." Macklin nodded toward a stark white structure with jutting lines and tall panes of glass.

"And I always thought Space Mountain was at Disneyland," she remarked sarcastically, sipping from the beer she had kept between her knees. Mordente tipped the beer toward a home coming up on their right. "Whose place is that?"

Macklin glanced over and felt his heartbeat pick up its pace. "That's Crocker Orlock's estate. You can tell by the heart-shaped swimming pool."

Mordente looked down at it as Macklin circled the estate. Three limousines were parked on the circular driveway that surrounded a stone fountain. Pillars of white water shot high into the air.

"That's quite a spread." Mordente nodded in appreciation at Orlock's large Georgian home with its Greek-style columns in the front. "It looks like an Athens tract home, you know what I mean?"

Macklin smiled.

"Have you ever seen his boat?" she asked.

"Nope. What's it like?"

"The Queen Mary."

They laughed, Macklin making a southward pass over the famed HOLLYWOOD sign and heading westward above the office buildings and condominium towers of the Wilshire Corridor.

"Ready to head back?"

Mordente shrugged. "Whatever you say, Captain."

"I say let's pick up two steaks and let me make us some dinner. How does that sound to the crew?"

She chuckled. "The crew will postpone the mutiny. For now."

CHAPTER THIRTEEN

"I didn't know men knew how to cook," she said, her eyes half closed, the gentle effect of the wine. Sitting close to Macklin on his couch, she wasn't sure if the warmth she felt was from the wine, the crackling fire, or him. Perhaps it was an enticing combination.

"They don't." He grinned. "The steak was real—everything else was Stouffer's." He felt childishly nervous, his heart fluttering like that of a teenage boy who was afraid his newfound deep voice would crack and reveal his uneasiness.

She looked into his eyes and laughed, the sound tickling him. It made him happy, and it made him guilty. Only three days had passed since Cheshire's death, and already he wanted another woman.

He held the gaze despite himself and she slipped her arm around him, sliding snugly against his side.

"I can't," he whispered, starting to rise. She grasped him tightly, holding him down.

"You can't what?" she replied softly. "All I did was put my arm around you."

Macklin chuckled self-consciously.

She grinned back at him and removed her arm from his shoulder. "Look, that was a stupid thing for me to say. I know you're feeling confused right now. So am I."

They stared into each other's eyes silently. Macklin needed to feel close to someone now, he needed someone to accept him as a loving human being and not as Mr. Jury. Her eyes offered a sanctuary from the world of violence he lived in.

She tentatively brushed his cheek with her fingers and leaned toward him uncertainly. Macklin tensed, repulsed and drawn to her at the same time. Her lips touched his with such tenderness that he couldn't stop himself from wrapping his arm around her and drawing her close.

His arm felt strong and assured to her, though the pounding heart she felt against her side hinted at his trepidation.

Macklin's kisses were light and uneasy, barely touching her lips. His conflicting emotions and the strength of his desire were dizzying. He was frightened. She understood, parting her lips slowly. But Macklin could sense the hunger in her breaths, in her gentle shivers. The sensuality of her response stoked his desire into an uncontrollable firestorm. His hand dropped to her breast, stroking it through her shirt. She made a luscious, soft sound and caressed his thigh, letting her hand drift tantalizingly close to his stiffening penis. He raised his hand slightly and undid the buttons of her shirt.

Mordente moaned, spreading her legs and leaning back against the couch. Her breasts tumbled out the wide V of her open blouse, the nipples aroused into hard points. Macklin dropped his head and, with deliberate slowness, kissed and sucked and licked his way down her chest, moving off the couch and leaning over her. She writhed, running her fingers through his hair, massaging his scalp. He molded his lips around the stem of her right nipple, teasing it with his moist tongue. She dragged her fingernails across his back, parting her legs wide and pushing herself against the bulge of his erection. They ground to a quickening rhythm.

Macklin slid one hand down her flat stomach to her belt, carefully unbuckling it. She felt his hot breath on her cleavage as he moved to her left nipple, already excited by his sucking of her other breast.

She pulled his shirt out of his pants and slipped her hands under the tight waistband and over his buttocks, soft and smooth to the touch. Macklin's erection pressed uncomfortably against his jeans.

Leaning back, Macklin yanked down her pants and she opened his, slipping down his briefs and wrapping her hand tightly around his penis. She looked into his eyes and smiled, pulling him to her. "Let me take *you* on a ride ..."

Noises that invaded Macklin's sleep always seemed ten times louder than they did when he was awake. That didn't change Sunday morning. When the phone rang, it sounded like a fire alarm going off next to his ear.

He grabbed for it angrily, nearly knocking the whole thing on the floor, where it would undoubtedly have crashed down like a two-ton boulder.

"Yes?" he whispered with aggravation, looking over his bare shoulder at Mordente, who lay on her left side with her naked back to him. His fingers traced the thin white lines left on her back by the straps of her bathing suit.

"It's me," Mort said. "The stuff is here and I've checked it out. It's fine. What the hell do you plan to do with it?"

Macklin picked up his watch on the nightstand and glanced at the time. Nine o'clock.

"I'll tell you when I get there, around two," Macklin mumbled, gently lifting up the sheet and admiring Mordente's firm buttocks and slim, crossed legs. "How are you feeling?"

"Better than you'd think." Mort laughed. "But I look like Quasimodo's uglier half-brother."

" 'Bye." Macklin set the phone down gently and slide close to Mordente, pressing himself against her back and slipping one hand between her legs.

She stirred, uncrossing her legs. Macklin nuzzled her neck and let his fingers explore her.

"Good morning," she said, her eyes still closed.

"Good morning," he echoed. "How are you?

"Fine." She grinned. "And getting better."

Macklin rolled over on top of her and gave her a deep kiss.

"But," she said, holding his face in her hands, "I've got work to do today, a free-lance story that must go to New York by Express Mail tomorrow morning."

Macklin kissed her again, stroking her between her legs with his forefinger.

"Maybe," she moaned, "it could wait for an hour or so."

The moment Macklin walked into the hangar, he could tell something was wrong. Mort was in the office sitting on Macklin's desk, holding the phone close to his ear, his brow furrowed.

"Brett, it's Shaw," Mort said, putting his hand over the mouthpiece. A large white bandage covered the side of his head. "All the equipment is in the chopper."

Macklin nodded and took the receiver from him. "Bad news?" he asked Shaw.

"Yep, I think Orlock skipped out on us this morning," Shaw said. "I'm trying to get a search warrant to go through the house, but it will take time. It's Sunday and all the judges are on the golf course."

"Shit, where is he?" He couldn't stand the idea of Orlock slipping through his fingers.

"That's a dumb question," Shaw snapped. "How the hell do I know? His lawyers say he's here but unavailable. I think it's bullshit and I can't get the law on my side to force its hand. The cogs of the legal machine move slowly on weekends."

The legal machine always works slowly, Macklin thought, if it even works at all. "Who is Orlock's lawyer?"

"Jules Baldwin, a young Century City type, the kind who works seven days a week," Shaw said.

Macklin glanced at Mort. There might be a way to find Orlock after all. "Orlock can't be far. Look, Ronny, don't you worry about it. I'll find out where he is." He gripped the receiver tightly. "You just get me the go-ahead from Harlan Fitz."

Shaw sighed. "I already did."

Jules Baldwin knew his wife didn't like the stainless steel-modern look of his new law office, the glass-walled corner of the fifth floor of a Century City tower. He didn't give a shit whether she liked it or not. The decor was one way of keeping the pain in the ass out of the office. He loved his work far more than he'd ever love his wife.

It was a $300-an-hour interior decorator, a woman he described to friends as "extremely fuckable," and a late-night rerun of UFO that had given him the inspiration for the office's sci-fi style. The hanging prints were all new wave splashes of color framed in silver against a white wall. The plants were potted in silver vases beside silver-wrought hi-tech chairs that Captain Kirk would be quite comfortable sitting in.

Baldwin sat in just such a chair, hunched over an ink-scrawled yellow legal pad that lay amidst a smattering of papers on his glass desk. Behind him was a window that afforded him a sweeping view of the Century Plaza Hotel.

He'd stare out the window at the hotel and console himself by thinking that though he didn't have a view like the other partners, he had Andrea for a secretary.

His mind had begun to wander to Friday's lunchtime dictation, which Andrea took between his legs, when the white phone rang and interrupted his pleasant memories.

"Jules Baldwin," he said, his New York upbringing turning Baldwin into Bowldwin as he spoke.

"Yeah, this is the garage," the caller drawled. "There's been an accident down here with your car."

Baldwin's eyebrows shot up and the color drained from his face. Images of his BMW 320i as a crumpled mass of twisted metal flashed in front of his eyes. "M-My car?" It came out "Cah." "My car? Shit, I'll be right down."

He slammed down the receiver and dashed out of his office.

Macklin, downstairs in the garage beside the bank of elevators, hung up the pay phone with a smile and waved to Mort, who sat behind the wheel of Macklin's idling Impala.

Macklin pressed his back to the wall beside the elevator door and waited. A second later, the doors parted and Baldwin rushed out. Macklin stuck out his leg.

Baldwin cried out, falling face first onto the cement. Macklin was on him in an instant, sitting on Baldwin's back and pinning back the lawyer's arms. Baldwin, his cheek to the cool cement, screamed out in terror as the Impala shot forward out of the shadows and closed in on him.

"Nooooooooo!" Baldwin cried shrilly. The Impala screeched to a stop two feet short of his head.

Baldwin panted, fear dampening his face with sweat.

"Where's Orlock?" Macklin demanded, twisting Baldwin's arm.

"Who's Orlock?" Baldwin yelled, the sound of the engine in his ears, the exhaust filling his nostrils. "I don't know anyone named Orlock."

The Impala jerked forward. Baldwin screamed and squeezed his eyes closed as the front end of the car passed over his head. He opened his eyes and stared into the tread of the left front tire, now inches from his face.

The engine growled above him.

"Tell me where Orlock is or they'll be wiping you up with a mop," Macklin hissed.

"On his boat. He's on his fucking boat, okay?" Baldwin exclaimed. "He's going to Costa Rica."

"Why?"

Baldwin was silent.

"Two seconds, scum, and you're dogshit on my tire."

The engine revved hungrily. "Okay, okay, he's gonna pull a Robert Vesco," Baldwin said, his voice cracking. "All his money is safe in Swiss banks, so he's running. He wants to be out of the country before the cops are able to get past me to him. He's going to disappear into South America and die a wealthy man."

"Not if I can help it." Macklin stood up, pulling Baldwin up with him. The lawyer's head smashed against the underside of the car. Baldwin let out a sharp, guttural cry of pain. Macklin lowered him a few inches and then suddenly yanked him up again. Baldwin's head hit the car with a metallic thud.

Macklin released Baldwin, leaving the dazed and limp lawyer shaking on the ground, and got into the car on the passenger side. Mort slipped the gear into reverse and sped backward out of the garage.

As unconsciousness closed in on Baldwin, he thanked God his car was all right after all.

CHAPTER FOURTEEN

B rett Macklin's helicopter streaked westward, chasing the setting sun across the Pacific's blue, frothy swells in search of Orlock's yacht, the *Profiteer.*

While Macklin peered out the window, scanning the ocean, Mort guided the chopper south of Catalina Island, which loomed several miles to their right against a purple sky.

"Brett, pretty soon it's going to be too dark," Mort said.

Macklin kept his eyes on the water skirting past them. "He's not going to slither away, Mort. We're going to find him."

"Maybe Baldwin lied. Maybe this is a wild goose chase."

"No, I can feel it. Orlock's out there."

"Where out there?" Mort groaned to himself.

Macklin heard him but made no comment. Orlock won't escape, Macklin thought. This time Orlock *will* pay for his crimes.

Macklin's eyes narrowed on a white dot in the distance. *Yes, it has to be.* He nudged Mort and pointed. "That's him."

"How can you be sure?"

Macklin slipped on the leather gloves in his lap. "I'm sure," he said, picking up a rifle from the floor.

He slid open the window and stared down the rifle's sight, following the one-hundred-foot yacht's wide wake to the stern, where he could see the word *Profiteer* behind a wet bike secured to the diving platform.

"All right, Mort, it's showtime," Macklin said with a grim smile. He strapped on a wide brown harness that had three carabiners, looped metal clasps, dangling from it.

Macklin had ordered the equipment from Shaw in case the law couldn't get near Orlock and Macklin would have to seek justice himself. The equipment was for an assault on Orlock's mansion. But, Macklin realized, the open sea was much better. No witnesses. No danger of being identified. No police to intrude.

"It's going to be tricky, Brett," Mort said. "He's going about twenty-five knots."

Macklin picked up the rifle again, sticking the barrel out the window and sighting the upper deck, close to the wheelhouse. "Then we'll just have to slow 'em down." He squeezed the trigger.

The tear gas canister burst out of the rifle and whistled down to the yacht, missing its target and hitting the launch crane. The smoking canister clattered to the deck floor and shrouded the yacht's stern in thick, eye-stinging fog.

"Damn," Macklin hissed, taking aim on the wheelhouse again. "Get me closer, Mort, and keep her steady."

A man emerged from the wheelhouse, firing a machine gun at the helicopter. Mort veered away, the machine gun a flickering spark on the *Profiteer*'s deck.

"No!" Macklin scolded Mort. "Stay on her ass."

Mort, realizing the futility of arguing, reluctantly brought the helicopter to bear on the yacht again. Macklin adjusted his aim, centering the sights on the turtleneck-clad gunman.

Macklin fired, the canister slamming the gunman through the wheelhouse window. A second later, billows of tear gas rose from the wheelhouse and the yacht slowed.

"Okay, let's get on top of them," Macklin said, dropping his rifle on the floor and opening the door. A burst of cold wind rushed into the helicopter, chilling their skin.

"Brett, are you sure you want to do this?" Mort asked.

Macklin ignored him, yelling over the whir of the chopper blades and the rush of sea air. "Bring her down as close as you dare over the stern, then get up and keep your eyes open."

Mort nodded. "Be careful, Brett."

Macklin smiled. "I will." He slipped a .44 Magnum automatic in his harness, pulled a gas mask over his head, and dropped one end of a nylon rope out the window. The rope spilled out, dangling seventy-five feet below the chopper and disappearing in the gas cloud on the *Profiteer*'s stern.

He snapped a carabiner to the rope, which ran through the metal loop on down between his legs. Holding the rope tightly, Macklin backed out of the helicopter, pausing with his body hunched outward and his feet planted firmly against the doorframe.

"You're crazy, Brett," Mort bellowed.

Macklin, straddling the rope, winked and pushed off. He slid down the rope quickly. He enjoyed the illusion of being stationary, the ocean raising the boat up to him, offering Orlock on a one-hundred-foot, narrow platter.

The rope suddenly ran out, slipping through his fingers. Macklin dropped through ten feet of thin air into the tear gas cloud. Without warning, he crashed onto the hardwood deck.

Macklin lay stunned, curled up on the deck, pain buzzing in his legs, fireworks bursting in his eyes. *So this is what it's like to be a raindrop.* The sound of bullets clamoring for him brought him to his senses. He tumbled like a breadroller along the floor, the bullets cutting a trail across the wood inches from his body.

He bolted to his feet and yanked out his .44 Magnum automatic in one motion, catching sight of a figure staggering in the greenish haze near the cabin directly ahead. Macklin squeezed the trigger, the Magnum spitting slugs through the smoke. The bullets hammered into the figure, skipping him across the floor like a hand-tossed stone skimming the surface of the water.

Macklin dashed to the cabin wall and pressed himself against it. His heart throbbed in his throat and he felt slightly queasy. A ticklish feeling pinned him to the wall for fifteen seconds. Fear. *C'mon, Ace Commando, you can't chicken out now.*

Taking a deep breath, he slid to his left toward the cabin door. He hesitantly reached out for the latch and pulled it open. No gunfire exploded through the doorway. That means nothing, Macklin thought. Whoever is inside might just be waiting to see the whites of my eyes.

Pivoting on his right foot, he spun in a crouch facing the open door, his gun ready. He saw a lavish living room, complete with piano, wet bar, plush couches, and dark wood bookcases lined with volumes. A stuffed swordfish was mounted, mid-jerk, on the wall above the bar. Pictures of Tinseltown pirates, from Errol Flynn to Robert Shaw, hung around the cabin.

Macklin entered the cabin slowly, moving toward the low door directly in front of him. He stepped down the two steps leading to it cautiously and thought about how much he hated closed doors and what they might hide. The abrasive sound of the chopper circling overhead was reassuring. At least he wasn't alone.

Pressing his shoulder to the door, he twisted the handle and burst into the dark passageway. He froze, listening for a sign of lurking danger. His face was hot in the gas mask, his warm breath trapped inside.

He crept slowly forward, waiting for someone to leap out of an adjoining room. An explosion behind him shook the passageway. A single split second of understanding, long enough for Macklin to realize a gun had been fired, preceded the two bullets. They pounded into his back, shoving him forward onto the floor. Flat on his stomach, his consciousness swirling and his body numb, he desperately tried to suck in breath as darkness closed in on him.

Mort buzzed above the yacht, worried. He hadn't seen any sign of Macklin for several minutes. That wasn't good. The tear gas had dissipated, and he could see the launch crane swinging out over the water, a single figure in the motorboat. It had to be Orlock.

Damn. Mort flashed on the front-mounted three-million-candle-power searchlight Stocker had stolen from an LAPD Air Support Unit allocation. A bright beam of light sliced the darkness and concentrated on the speedboat slapping the surface. A man in a yellow life vest cowered in the light, unclasping the launch ties.

Orlock—it had to be Orlock. Mort switched on the loudspeaker.

"You're not going anywhere, Orlock," Mort's voice boomed down from the sky. Orlock settled behind the wheel and twisted the key, the outboard motor sputtering to life.

"Damnit," Mort said to himself in frustration. "Where's Brett?"

The launch sped away from the yacht, cutting a sharp swath in the water.

"Orlock is escaping in the launch," Mort barked into the mike, following the boat with the searchlight.

Macklin lay motionless in the passageway, Mort's words vaguely registering in his throbbing head. He felt the floor shudder under the weight of approaching footsteps. Macklin steadied his breathing, willing his head to clear.

The footsteps stopped. A hand gripped Macklin's shoulder and turned him over. Macklin pumped three shells into the man's gut. Blood burst out the man's back, splattering the walls.

The gunman staggered back, blood bubbling from his stomach, his face drawn into an expression of confused surprise. His half-closed eyes asked *How?*

"Flak jacket, asshole," Macklin hissed, driving his foot into the man's bloody midsection. The man's face bloated and his stomach imploded with a squish, swallowing Macklin's foot.

The man toppled backward and Macklin heard the wet slurp of his foot being released. The body landed with a dull splash in the puddle of blood.

Macklin sat up slowly, his back rigid with pain from the impact of bullets into the flack jacket concealed under his jumpsuit.

Reaching out to the wall for support, Macklin was able to pull himself into a standing position. He stepped around the gunman's corpse and forced himself to move quickly back up the steps, through the main cabin, and out onto the deck.

Yanking off his gas mask, Macklin turned to his right and saw his helicopter hovering above him, its searchlight trained on a motorboat racing through the night toward Catalina.

"Are you all right?" Mort blared from the helicopter.

Macklin waved and then pointed frantically in the direction of the speeding launch. *Go after him!* After a second or two of hovering, Mort got the message and veered away in pursuit of Orlock.

Orlock mustn't make it to Catalina and contact the authorities, Macklin thought, suddenly remembering the wet bike he had spied in his rifle sights earlier.

Macklin leaned over the stern and saw the wet bike, an oceanfaring version of a motorcycle, secured to the fantail. Glancing over his shoulder as he leaped onto the platform, he could see the launch swerving as the helicopter snaked in and out of Orlock's path.

I hope Mort can slow him down, Macklin thought, untying the wet bike. If Orlock made it to the island, Macklin knew the authorities would place Orlock in protective custody. Orlock would relax safely in the taxpayers' care while sympathetic publicity casting him as a victim raged in the media and muted the city's chances of putting Orlock behind bars on kiddie porn charges.

Macklin's back screamed with pain as he bent down and lifted the wet bike, bracing his legs to take most of the weight. *What if Orlock saw the call letters on the chopper?* The thought teased Macklin as he lowered the wet bike onto the water and straddled it. Orlock could end up remaining free while Macklin faced a lifetime in prison for murder.

The wet bike jerked forward and skipped across the swells toward the launch, which sped in a curving path under the bright searchlight of the low-flying helicopter.

That's it, Mort, pin him down. Macklin twisted the throttle, urging the wet bike forward. Cool mist splashed his face and whipped his hair.

The helicopter swooped down on Orlock, who frantically twisted the wheel and brought the launch around, crossing Macklin's path. Orlock noticed his pursuer for the first time. Macklin could see Orlock's wild, enraged face in the white light, his teeth gritted and his eyes wide.

Macklin closed in on Orlock's boat, his wet bike bouncing violently in the choppy water kicked up by the spinning helicopter blades and the converging wakes from the circuitous path cut by Orlock's outboard motor. A loud mechanical grind, the cacophony of engines, grated against Macklin's ears.

Macklin's one chance to stop Orlock came in an instant. Orlock swerved to avoid the chopper and momentarily came alongside the wet bike. Macklin threw himself into the boat. The Magnum slipped out of Macklin's harness into the ocean as he bashed painfully against the edge of the boat and tumbled inside.

Orlock abandoned the wheel and pounced on Macklin. The boat spun out of control. Orlock fell forward onto Macklin and they rolled toward the stem. Macklin, dazed and disoriented, felt Orlock's chilly hands squeeze his neck, cutting off his air.

Lifting Macklin by the neck, Orlock draped him over the back of the boat beside the growling outboard and forced his head down to the water. Macklin reached out, scratching and pulling at Orlock's face. But it was no good. The cold water rushed up Macklin's nostrils as Orlock pushed his head under. Macklin's head pounded, deprived of air, and he could feel the deadly motion of the rotor blades buzzing an inch from his left ear.

Macklin grabbed the boat with his right hand and pressed the palm of his left hand under Orlock's chin, trying to push him back. Time was working against Macklin. The lack of air was weakening him, and Orlock was edging Macklin's head to the rotor, now so close Macklin could feel the blade skimming past his ear.

Frantic, his chest swelled with agony, Macklin slapped the outboard with his left hand. He felt the rotor blade slice at strands of his hair. His fingers fell on the gearshift and he yanked it down.

The boat jolted into reverse, the momentum jerking Macklin forward. Macklin used the split-second advantage, ramming his knee into Orlock's groin. The momentum, combined with the blow, knocked Orlock off balance.

Orlock tumbled over Macklin and splashed into the water beside the back-circling boat. Macklin pulled himself up, heaving, each breath a razor-sharp dagger plunged down his throat. Water streamed down Macklin's icy blue face.

Looking back, Macklin saw Orlock bobbing in turbulent waters, and he flipped the gearshift up. The boat kicked forward and Macklin scrambled to the wheel.

He pushed the throttle lever forward and gunned the boat, bringing it around in a wide circle and bearing down on Orlock, who bobbed like a buoy ahead.

"No!" Orlock screamed, trying to dive, the vest keeping him afloat.

Macklin kept coming, seeing only the murdered children and Orlock's grand estate.

Make them pay!

The launch ripped through Orlock, tearing his body apart in a crimson splash of water.

EPILOGUE

Jessica Mordente felt edgy and uncomfortable when she emerged from Cock V Bull, an English-style buffet fronting the west edge of the Sunset Strip. The feeling had begun when Chet picked her up at her apartment and continued unabated through their empty dinner conversation and her forced light-hearted repartee.

Navarro came up behind her, chewing on a toothpick, and put his arm around her shoulder. "What happened to the old Jessica Mordente?"

"Why? What does she have that I don't?" she asked, walking with Navarro away from the restaurant. She shouldn't be mad at him, she knew. After all, she had been the one to ask him out on Friday and he'd been affable all evening. But with each moment spent with him, her uneasiness intensified.

"An appetite, for one." He removed his arm and shoved his hands into his pockets. "You used to eat everything in there except the table. Tonight you barely were able to stomach your crumpet."

Mordente shrugged. "I dunno, I just wasn't hungry. I've been working pretty hard and snacking all day." She knew that wasn't it, though. It was that sense of impending doom that had been hanging over her like a dark storm cloud.

"And item two," he continued, stopping beside his sleek, white Pontiac Fiero. "I usually have to dodge ten zillion questions from you. That would irritate most sane people, but not me. I like that about you, that mix of a sharklike predatory instinct coupled with a dash of good-natured inquisitiveness. It's fun in a masochistic sort of way."

He flashed a playful grin at her. "Now you're a sissy. I don't get it."

"C'mon, Chet, take it easy on me," she sighed. "I'm sorry. You've tried very hard and it's been a pleasant evening. I guess you're right. I'm not myself tonight."

Navarro unlocked the car and opened the door. "Maybe this will bring you back to your senses." He reached behind the seat and pulled out a manila envelope, then turned and held it out to her.

"Here's one of the photographs taken by the bank camera," he said, looking at her sternly. "This is strictly off the record, understand? You can look at it, but that's it."

Mordente nodded expressionlessly and took the envelope.

"To be honest," he continued, "we see no reason to go after the guy, you know?"

She lifted the flab and pulled out the photo.

"Not a bad picture, huh?" he asked.

"Crystal clear," she muttered, her throat dry. Brett Macklin's piercing gaze was unmistakable.

AFTERWORD

The creation of Brett Macklin—and "Ian Ludlow"—is explained in this essay, published as a "My Turn" column in Newsweek magazine in 1985. Pinnacle Books went out of business before the fourth novel in the series was set to be published.

HOT SEX, GORY VIOLENCE

How One Student Earns Course Credit and Pays Tuition

My name is Ian Ludlow. Well, not really. But that's the name on my four *.357 Vigilante* adventures that Pinnacle Books will publish this spring. Most of the time I'm Lee Goldberg, a mild-mannered UCLA senior majoring in mass communications and trying to spark a writing career at the same time. It's hard work. I haven't quite achieved a balance between my dual identities of college student and hack novelist.

The adventures of Mr. Jury, a vigilante into doing the LAPD's dirty work, are often created in the wee hours of the night, when I should be studying, meeting my freelance-article deadlines, or, better yet, sleeping. More often than not, my nocturnal writing spills over into my classes the next morning. Brutal fistfights, hot sexual encounters, and gory violence are frequently scrawled across my anthropology notes or written amid my professor's insights on Whorf's hypothesis. Students sitting next to me who glance at my lecture notes are shocked to see notations like "Don't move, scumbag, or I'll wallpaper the room with your brains."

I once wrote a pivotal rape scene during one of my legal-communications classes, and I'm sure the girl who sat next to me thought I was a psychopath. During the first half of the lecture, she kept looking with wide eyes from my notes to my face as if my nose were melting onto my binder or something. At the break she disappeared, and I didn't see her again the rest of the quarter. My professors, though, seem pleased to see me sitting in the back of the classroom writing furiously. I guess they think I'm hanging on their every word. They're wrong.

I've tried to lessen the strain between my conflicting identities by marrying the two. Through the English department, I'm getting academic credit for the books. That amazes my grandpa Cy, who can't believe there's a university crazy enough to reward me for writing "lots of filth." The truth is, it's writing and it's learning, and it's getting me somewhere. Just where, I'm not sure. My grandpa Cy thinks it's going to get me the realization I should join him in the furniture business.

I don't admit to many people that I'm writing books. It sounds so pompous, arrogant, and phony when you say that in Los Angeles. See, everybody in Los Angeles is writing a book or screenplay. Walk into any 7-Eleven, tell the clerk you're an agent or a producer, and he'll whip out a handwritten, 630-page epic he's been keeping under the register for a chance like this.

I do involve my closest friends in the secret world of Ian Ludlow. When I finished writing my first sex scene, I made six copies and passed them around for a critique. I felt like I was distributing pornography. "How do you compliment a sex scene?" a girl I know complained. "It's embarrassing." Another friend rewrote the scene so it sounded like a cross between a beating and extensive surgery.

Among my family and even my friends, I find myself constantly apologizing for what I'm doing. Maybe I wouldn't if I were writing a Larry McMurtry or John Updike book. But I know what this is. This is a black cover with a rugged hero in the forefront, shoving a massive gun into the reader's face. I feign disgust, mutter something about "a guy's got to break in somehow," and quickly change the subject.

But the truth is, it's fun. And since Ian Ludlow is the guy who will take the heat for it, I can let myself relax and enjoy it. I'm building on those childhood hours spent in front of my mom's ancient Smith Corona, banging out hokey tales about superspies and supervillains. My work is still hokey, except now someone is paying me for it. And paying me not badly, either. I can pay for a whole year of college from the advances for the four novels.

The opportunity came my way thanks to Lewis Perdue, a journalism professor who writes those bulky conspiracy thrillers and harbors dreams of being the next Robert Ludlum. I used to read his manuscripts and debate the merits of Lawrence Sanders and Ken Follett. Then, when Pinnacle asked him to do an "urban man's action-adventure series," he passed it on to me. Pretty soon I was buying books like *The Butcher*, *The Executioner*, *The Penetrator*, *The Destroyer*, and *The Terminator* by the armful and flipping through the latest issues of *Soldier of Fortune* and *Gung-Ho*. After a week or two of wading through this, I was ready to spill blood across my home computer screen.

There's a part of me that doesn't like what I'm doing. It lectures me while I'm making some bad guy eat hot lead. It tells me I should be writing a novel about relationships and feelings, about the problems my peers are facing. *I will*, I say to myself, *later. There's plenty of time.*

ABOUT THE AUTHOR

Lee Goldberg is a two-time Edgar Award and two-time Shamus Award nominee and the #1 *New York Times* bestselling author of more than forty novels, including the *Eve Ronin* series, fifteen *Monk* novels, eight *Diagnosis Murder* novels, and five novels co-authored with Janet Evanovich. He has also written and/or produced many TV shows, including *Diagnosis Murder*, *SeaQuest*, and *Monk*, and he is the cocreator of the *Mystery 101* series of Hallmark movies. As an international television consultant, he has advised networks and studios in Canada, France, Germany, Spain, China, Sweden, and the Netherlands on the creation, writing, and production of episodic television series. He's also the founder of the publishing companies Brash Books and Cutting Edge Books. You can find more information about Lee and his work at www.leegoldberg.com.

www.ingramcontent.com/pod-product-compliance
Lightning Source LLC
Chambersburg PA
CBHW030131260626
47156CB00008B/2890